GOING DOWN
FOR THE
COUNT

Books by David Stukas

SOMEONE KILLED HIS BOYFRIEND

GOING DOWN FOR THE COUNT

Published by Kensington Publishing Corporation

GOING DOWN FOR THE COUNT

David Stukas

KENSINGTON BOOKS
http://www.kensingtonbooks.com

KENSINGTON BOOKS are published by

Kensington Publishing Corp.
850 Third Avenue
New York, NY 10022

All Kensington titles, imprints and distributed lines are available at special quantity discounts for bulk purchases for sales promotion, premiums, fundraising, educational or institutional use.

Special book excerpts or customized printings can also be created to fit specific needs. For details, write or phone the office of the Kensington Special Sales Manager: Kensington Publishing Corp., 850 Third Avenue, New York, NY, 10022. Attn. Special Sales Department. Phone: 1-800-221-2647.

Kensington and the K logo Reg. U.S. Pat. & TM Off.

Library of Congress Card Catalogue Number: 2001099500
ISBN 0-7582-0039-0

First Printing: August 2002
10 9 8 7 6 5 4 3 2 1

Printed in the United States of America

To Gary Stanton, mastermind,
To Rainer and Georg, meine Freunde,
To John, my extraordinary editor,
And to Jack, always Jack.

1

Stand By Your Man

When Count Siegfreid von Schmidt, one of the richest, handsomest, and most openly gay men in Germany, fell madly in love with me, my friends couldn't believe it—especially my dearest. Monette, my lesbian friend, was naturally very happy for me, but insanely jealous, also. This probably explains why she stated—and I quote her—that she must have been sucked through a wormhole in the space-time continuum and come out in a wacky, parallel universe where nothing made sense. I made a mental note to get back at her in a completely childish manner at a later date.

My other best friend, the gorgeous, chronically untalented, and sex-crazed heir to a herpes-ointment fortune, Michael Stark, had a different reaction. He laughed. And laughed. And laughed. In fact, he laughed so hard he lost a cap from one of his meticulously polished teeth.

But in all sincerity, I was the most stunned. *Who, me?* I thought, looking around at everyone but myself. *Me?* I had a right to be skeptical, after all. In fact, not just a right, but a proven track record.

Rich, handsome, internationally traveled, and cultured are not the sort of terms normally used to describe my dates. Mine were mostly 3-D: drunk, drugged, or desperate. Did I mention psychotic or mentally crippled?

But it was true. The count and I were seen everywhere around New York, eating in trendy restaurants, dancing in cutting-edge clubs. Yes, my life had turned around from tear-inducing boredom to jet set in a matter of weeks. Everything was going my way.

If it weren't for his dead body lying with his head in a toilet, a knife in his back, and me being the last person to see him alive, I wouldn't have had a thing to complain about.

When I began to think how I got into this situation, I had to look back in a vain attempt to unravel the whole mess. It didn't take long, however, since the two largest crises in my life had one thing in common: my friend Michael Stark. The man could provoke disaster in my life from three states away. In fact, I can blame him with complete assurance for getting me into the largest fiascos of my existence. This particular one started when I was having dinner at a very nice restaurant with Michael in my adopted city of New York.

". . . so this guy takes out this rubber chicken and starts beating this guy up with it. Whack! Whack! The guy's back was covered with big, purple bruises and he was loving every minute of it," Michael spouted breathlessly, recounting a scene at a sex party he'd recently attended. "It was so perverse. You wanted to laugh. The guy on the receiving end didn't do much laughing, though."

"Michael, please, I'm eating . . . a rubber chicken?" I asked, weirdly interested.

"Yes!" Michael said excitedly. "Pretty wild, huh?"

"Michael, I know your sexual tastes and mine are a little different," I started, but was cut off at the pass.

"You mean I get it on a regular basis?" Michael added cattily.

"If you mean *hourly*, Michael, then you're correct. By the

way, what's keeping you from pillowing the waiter? After all, we've been here over an hour."

"He's not my type."

"I thought any carbon-based life-form with a large you-know-what was your type."

"Well, at least I *have* sex, Robert. I think the wives of Wall Street investment bankers get it more often than you do."

"That's because they're paying for it," I protested.

"Maybe you're on to something. Yeah . . . the solution to all your problems, Robert! Pay! If you did, you'd be guaranteed to have sex. I know some escorts who would be perfect for you. They could dress up like a Catholic bishop and have sex with you. Or they could watch you organize your apartment while they jerked off."

"Make fun all you want just because I'm not as kinky as you, Michael. I'm more of the romantic type. You know—soft music, champagne, candles."

"That reminds me. I saw the most fascinating hot-wax demonstration on this incredibly hunky guy at the Bound for Glory Bondage Club last Thursday night."

"Michael, I'm trying to be romantic and you're talking about dripping candle wax on some naked guy at some sleazy sex club where the term 'groin pull' takes on a whole new meaning!"

"Yeah, and?" Michael asked, incredulous that I thought there was something wrong with the scene he had just described. Michael was very muscular, gorgeous, rich, popular, vain, and unbelievably selfish. But above all, sex was what blew air up Michael's skirt. "The reason why you can't bed a guy—any guy—is that you're so sexually repressed. Guys don't want to date the Pope. You can talk all the romance shit you want, but you prove your worth in bed, believe me."

"Michael, you've been on more mattresses than the quality control guy at Sealy Posturpedic. Just you wait. As traditional as my values may be . . ." I started.

". . . prehistoric is more like it," Michael added.

I brushed Michael's comments aside and continued, ". . . they'll help me snag some guy who believes love is very much alive. A guy who wants to spend afternoons walking along the beach, watching old black-and-white movies, or sharing a good book."

Michael began grimacing as if I had just asked him to picture Donald Trump naked.

"That's right, Michael, *r-o-m-a-n-c-e*. It's all about being with someone and looking up at the stars at night . . ." I tried to continue, but was cut off by a stunningly handsome man at the next table who seemed to be finishing my sentences for me.

". . . and picnics in the woods on a warm spring day, poking through old junk stores on a Saturday afternoon, and a glass of wine while overlooking the Amalfi coast of Italy. Excuse me for eavesdropping on your conversation, but I couldn't help myself. I feel exactly the same way. My name is Count Siegfried von Schmidt. I didn't want to seem impertinent, but what you said touched something in my heart. I am looking for a man who feels old-fashioned love is not dead. That love is measured not by what you do in bed together, but by the time you spend with each other. How do you Americans say? The quality time. I feel there is more to be gained by spending an evening just staring into the embers crackling in a fireplace on a frosty autumn night with a lover than a thousand nights of sex."

Before I knew what was happening, Michael was circling his newfound prey.

"My name is Michael Stark, and I think what you said is completely wrong. I'll be happy to show you exactly how wrong you are," he said, almost peeling the clothing off the count with his words.

I don't know what got into me, but instead of abdicating

my tenuous romance with this mystery man to Michael like so many before, I ran to my battle station.

"Michael, I think the count was talking to *me*. You see, he seems to be more interested in romance that leaves a person with a sense of personal and spiritual fulfillment, not some baffling urinary tract infection."

"We'll let the count decide, shall we?" Michael added, figuring his handsome face and muscular body would certainly steal the count's affections.

"Actually, I don't want to create discord among two who are obviously very great friends. But I would like to give my phone number to this marvelous gentleman here," the count said, gesturing toward me with his Rolex-clad arm.

"Are you sure you don't want me? Guys always prefer me. Always!" Michael replied, his voice suddenly reeking with desperation.

"You are very handsome and have the kind of body that definitely excites me. But it is your friend here I am most interested in."

Suddenly, my world didn't make sense anymore. This couldn't be happening. Then it dawned on me: this had to be one of the extremely elaborate practical jokes my lesbian friend Monette played on me—and vice versa. I decided to test the waters.

"Did Monette put you up to this?" I asked.

"Monette? I don't know what you mean."

He seemed genuinely baffled by my request. Of course, it was difficult to tell completely, since the count was wearing dark sunglasses. His signature, I suppose. Or a way of fending off the flashes of paparazzi cameras I imagined were a fact of life for a person with a title—if he was indeed a real count.

"Never mind," I said, feeling it was safe to proceed.

"Here is my card, and I will write my cellular phone number on it so you may contact me." He scribbled some numbers on a beautiful business card with a fountain pen that had obviously been owned by some countess or czarina. Yup, *Count Siegfried von Schmidt* it said right on the card. And two German phone numbers: one in Berlin and the other in Hamburg.

"Now, I have shown you mine. Please show me yours," he said with complete innocence. Or did he?

Michael piped in, never losing a chance to vanquish a competitor. "You don't want to see *his*. It would take a particle accelerator just to get a glimpse of it."

"Thank you very much, Michael," I replied, not knowing if it was a good idea to hit Michael in the face with the empty wine bottle that sat on our table. Too many witnesses . . . plus, it wouldn't make the best impression on the count. "For your information, if the count wanted to see yours, he could just rent any porn video from Mammoth Films!"

"C'mon, Robert, you know for a fact I only made *one* porn film as a lark."

"Then why did *Battering Ram* have three sequels?" I queried Michael, not letting him off easily.

"I only starred in the first one, Robert. The other two were just cameo roles," Michael responded.

The count merely smiled. Although his English was almost perfect, I couldn't tell if he was being diplomatic and had decided not to get in the middle of our catfight, or if he didn't quite understand what was going on between Michael and me.

"I don't know what your plans are, but I would like to see you tomorrow," the count gently begged.

"Well, let me see . . ." I said, trying to create the impression of having a busy and demanding social schedule.

"He's probably going to a mesmerizing exhibit on book jacket covers at the New York Library," Michael interjected, managing to throw one more punch before the bell rang.

Actually, I was going to hear a lecture by Amanda Preistly, best-selling author of *Go Fuck Yourself—A Single Person's Guide to Having Sex with the Most Important Person in the*

World: You! But in light of the fact that I had a live man interested in me, I decided to forego dragging the count to a
book lecture about masturbation as the only orgasmic alter-
native to those who didn't have the six-figure income to pay
for love. If I wasn't going to inform the count about my
plans, I certainly wasn't about to let Michael know them.

"I can rearrange a few things," I finally relented. "Yes, I'd
like to see you very much. It would be an honor."

"Good. I would like to take you to a lecture. Gordon
Kuzuleekas is speaking about his latest novel. It's about a
group of Lithuanian intelligencia fleeing czarist Russia and
emigrating to America in the early 1900s. On their way to
America, however, they enter a hole in the space-time continuum and find themselves in a futuristic world populated
by robots. It promises to be quite engaging."

"I'd love to go," I gushed. I would go see a documentary
on the love life of Supreme Court Justice Ruth Bader Gins-
burg if the count asked me.

"I will call on you tomorrow. Ten o'clock. Yes?"

"That's perfect . . . Count," I stumbled, not knowing
what to call him.

"Siegfreid, please."

"Siegfreid it is. Ten o'clock."

"Until then," he said. He got up from his table and left
the restaurant, leaving an air of mystery and intrigue in his
wake. I was in love! Maybe this was the way life really was
supposed to be. Years of horrific dates that ended with
stolen wallets, a stubborn skin rash, and vomit on my favorite bathroom rug—and then love walks in the door. And
not just any love, but royalty.

"He's not going to call you back!" Michael blurted out,
trying to club my dreams to death.

"Michael, *he's* the one who made the advances. I didn't
ask him to talk to me. You can't stand the fact that he's interested in me and that you've finally run into a man you
can't have . . . no, worse—who doesn't want you."

"That's why I think he's a psycho. Any sane man would want me."

This comment was typical for Michael. He was the most egotistical, selfish, shallow, oversexed, wealthiest, and handsomest gay man I knew. He also got me into a lot of gay society events I could never get invited to on my own. His personality could best be summed up as toxic, but I didn't look a gift horse in the mouth, either. "He seems pretty normal to me, Michael . . . except for the 'count' thing."

"I tell you, Robert, the refrigerator in his hotel suite is full of frozen, decapitated heads, and he wants yours next. I've seen it all the time. These lunatics come across real suave and charming. They have expensive clothes, business cards, accents, and some of them act like they have some sort of connection to royalty. They look so normal, people don't stop to think for a minute that there could be anything wrong with them. The thing is, they prey on desperate people like you. They'll wine you, dine you, then take you back to their hotel or apartment and . . . skeeek!" Michael ran a finger across his throat for extra emphasis. "The next thing you know, the police break into the place and find you next to the frozen peas."

Whether Michael truly meant to protect me or not, he succeeded in planting the seed of doubt in my mind. Landing on the fertile ground of my paranoia and low self-esteem, the doubt grew like Japanese kudzu vine landing in a tub of plant fertilizer. I went from seeing love on the horizon to seeing meat cleavers. Maybe I was too trusting, but growing up in the Midwest hadn't taught me a lot about the world. "Do you really think he's a psycho impostor?" I asked anxiously.

"Of course he is. How many German counts have you run into during your lifetime? I've had sex with a lot of guys in Europe, and I still haven't run into one German count," Michael said proudly. "Well, there was one *head* in Europe who was pretty well crowned."

"I don't want to know about it. So are you sure about the count, Michael?"

"Absolutely."

"No doubts?"

"None whatsoever."

"So what am I supposed to do? He's going to call me tomorrow and will want to take me out."

"Just screen the calls on your answering machine and don't pick up the phone. Ignore him. You didn't give him your address, did you?"

"No."

"Good. I'm having a thing with a cop right now. Give me the count's phone number and I can have the sergeant do a check on him," Michael instructed, reaching over the table for me to hand him Siegfreid's business card.

"Your fuck buddy is a police sergeant?"

"No, he's a lieutenant. But he's known as The Sergeant."

"Michael, this guy doesn't have sex with you in uniform, does he?"

"Of course he does! Even better than a man out of uniform is a man in one. So give me the card and I'll have Sarge do a background check on him."

I reached out to hand the count's card to Michael. Then it struck me. I had just been slapped in the face and I almost didn't realize it. I pictured myself turning into the buffoon in one of those early Warner Brothers cartoons where the intellectually challenged character gets tricked and turns momentarily into a human-sized sucker. If that wasn't enough, the word *sucker* appeared across the character to further drum in the fact someone had been taken advantage of.

"Oh, no, you don't, you horndog," I said, snatching the count's business card back. "You tried to trick me into giving you his business card and I almost fell for it! You were going to get his phone number, call him up, and try to steal him away from me! You rotten little treacherous, backstabbing . . ." I said, trying to find the proper expletive to describe Michael.

"Robert, I can explain!" Michael tried to get in, but I was too darned mad.

"Slut! You common little slut!"

"That does it! Yes, I was going to steal him away from you, a man who once saved my life, but I am not going to sit here and have you call me common!" He stood up so abruptly his chair flew across the room and slammed into another patron's chair. No apologies were offered.

"I'm sorry I called you a common little slut. Actually, you're a trailer-trash slut!" I said loudly—perhaps a bit too loudly for a fashionable restaurant (Michael never ate in anything but).

"I'm leaving. You and your fucking Count Gorgeous can go off to fucking Romania and live happily every after!"

"Germany! He's from Germany! See, you don't even care where he's from! Go on, before I call McDonald's and tell them you've served more men than they have!" I shouted, realizing I *was* in a fashionable restaurant. Or, to be exact, was in a certain fashionable restaurant for the last time.

Michael stormed out of the place, leaving me sitting there with two thoughts on my mind once I calmed down. One, I was wondering if there was a magazine on bestiality and how many subscriptions I would send to Michael. And two, how, as an underpaid advertising copywriter, I was going to pay the one-hundred sixty-five dollars and thirty-seven-cents bill.

The next day, I woke up trying to justify my anger. Being a guilt-ridden Catholic (is there any other kind?), I made excuses for feeling the way I did. But no ifs, ands, or buts about it, Michael had confessed he was trying to steal the count for himself. And it wasn't the first time he had done so, either.

"Can you believe the gall of that vacuous, self-absorbed slag?" I blurted into the phone to Monette, my best friend in the world. In light of Michael's traitorous behavior, Monette had risen to the top of my list from the number-two position. Michael had previously been number one only because he let me use his house on Fire Island and invited me to his frequent cocktail parties populated by his buff-and-bluff friends.

"You don't need to come to me for confirmation, Robert. Michael has only one thing on his mind, and that's Michael. Er, and sex. OK, two things on his mind."

"So you think I should see this count guy?"

"No, Robert, I think you should bypass a possible real-life German count who sounds like the only sane gay man left on earth and go out on the streets and drag home another pathetic loser like the kind that are running loose in this city."

"No, but do you think he's for real?" I asked.

"Who cares?" Monette advised. "He seems genuinely interested in you. And you said he looks wealthy. What's not to like?"

"But what if he tries to stab me?"

"Look, Robert, if you don't date him, *I* will. And I'm a lesbian. A serious lesbian. What's wrong with you? You walk around desperate enough to take just about anything on two legs, the man of your dreams walks into your life, wants to sweep you off your feet—and you can't decide whether to go out with him! He's handsome, polished, and he's so good that Michael is frantically trying to get his hands on him. That should tell you how good you've got it. What have you got to lose?"

"My head, maybe."

"What?"

"Never mind."

"Go out with him, see where it leads, and call me back and give me all the details."

"OK, but if I don't come back, his phone number is . . ."

Monette knew me all too well. "Stop catastrophizing, Robert. He's not going to kill you, the slightly irregular-shaped vitamin you swallowed this morning was not a cyanide tablet put in your cupboard by an Iraqi terrorist, and a meteorite is not going to fall out of the sky and hit you while you're walking down 86th Street. My goddess, you have the most overactive imagination. You should become a writer and put your feverish brain to better use."

"OK, you've talked me into it. I'll go out with him. And I'll call you tomorrow morning."

"Not too early on Sunday. I'm going to a relationship workshop."

"But, Monette, you don't have relationships," I protested.

"Yeah, but I want to be ready when one stumbles along. Dr. Lydia Katz is giving this workshop."

"Not *the* Lydia Katz?" I exclaimed.

"Yes, why?"

"You're going to a workshop held by a lesbian who just got into a well-publicized slugfest with her girlfriend at a local restaurant?"

"I think this demonstrates that *all* couples could use a little counseling now and then," Monette said defensively.

"I think that it demonstrates Lydia ought to pick on someone her own size. The story in the local gay rags all said the girlfriend was over six-and-a-half feet tall. Lydia looked like a piece of hamburger when her girlfriend was through with her. She should have thought about that before she threw the first punch."

"Well, have a good time and call me!" Monette finished.

I hung up the phone, and before I had time to think about my impending date, my impending date called.

"Hello, this is Robert Willsop."

"Count von Schmidt here. Good morning, Robert, and how are you today? Did you have a nice dinner with your friend Michael?"

"It was OK."

"Just OK?"

"Oh, it was very nice," I said evasively, not wanting the count to know pleasantries would no longer be exchanged with Michael from now on—just gunfire.

"Marvelous! So," he said, with an authoritative abruptness that seemed so characteristically German. I found it very decisive and sexy. "How would you like to meet me for breakfast, er, brunch—is that the word?"

"I would love to. Yes, brunch would be nice."

"Excellent. Instead of attending the book lecture like we planned, I was wondering if you would accompany me to the Museum of Modern Art. There is an exhibit on the works of Kurt Schwitters. I collect his works."

A man who had *real* art! I was in love! The closest I came to collecting art was buying posters of Monet's overhyped water lilies. It was hard to imagine—a man who collected the works of internationally famous artists was interested in me!

I pictured myself on his private Gulfstream V jet, flying from international capital to international capital. Villas in Italy, schlosses (is that the plural for schloss?) in his native land, chalets in the Alps. Auctions in London! I could see myself holding up my own little auction paddle, driving up the stakes for a priceless thirteenth-century Italian lute into the stratosphere.

"Oh, honey," I would say to the count in hushed tones, "don't you think it would look good over the sofa in our palace in Berlin?"

There would be gasps in the crowd as I held my ground against a sheik who was determined to have the lute at any price. Eventually, the sheik would relent at sixteen million

American dollars, knowing his oil fortunes couldn't match those of the von Schmidts (of which I was legally now one—I had my name changed from Willsop to that of the count's after our marriage in Holland).

"Robert? Are you there?" the count asked.

"Oh . . . why, yes! I guess my mind wandered off. Forgive me, Count! Could you repeat what you just said?"

"First, breakfast, then museum."

"Sounds terrific."

"There is this restaurant that interests me. F/E/2, I think it is called."

I didn't have the nerve to tell the count he probably wouldn't get in. It was *the* hip restaurant of the moment. They reportedly even had Nanina Fabrique, the stellar super-supermodel, waiting at the bar for over an hour and five minutes last week. This was no mean feat, since her temper tantrums were legendary and expensive. Her last destructive stay at the Four Seasons had cost her in excess of seventy-six thousand dollars, a fact she merely shrugged off and earned back in a mere five minutes posing next to a bottle of overpriced perfume.

"I would like very much to see this place while I am in America. Can you be there in one hour?"

I can be there in five minutes, I thought, but decided I needed the time to accomplish a very important mission. "One hour is fine. I will see you there."

As soon as I hung up the phone, I ran to my computer and turned it on. Within minutes, I was on the Internet searching the web for anything on Count Siegfreid von Schmidt. And lo and behold, there he was. I couldn't read everything, since some websites were in German, but there were pictures galore. Here in a ponytail, there with his head shaved, different clothes, and always the dark glasses. There was no doubt about it—I had a real live German count in love with me.

I turned off the computer and sat there staring at the darkened screen. This just couldn't be happening to me. It was too surreal. I felt like I was on the verge of my life taking off in the direction it was supposed to be heading. I wasn't meant to drudge for an advertising agency all my life, or live in a crummy studio apartment. I was intelligent and fairly knowledgeable of what was going on in New York. Why did so many empty-headed, worthless people live in the lap of luxury when clearly it was I who deserved to? Maybe it was my time to be rewarded for sticking to my guns and not sleeping my way to the top.

I put on my best pair of jeans, a dark polo shirt, and slipped on some moccasins without socks—my I'm-metropolitan-but-I-don't-have-to-show-it outfit. It was the best I could do on my limited budget.

I arrived at the restaurant, but the count was nowhere to be seen. I scanned the throng begging to be admitted, but no count. Maybe he'd rethought the matter and decided to stand me up. It wouldn't be the first time.

I'd waited for ten minutes when I felt a hand on my shoulder. It was the count's.

"There you are, dear Robert. I have been waiting at the table for you. I thought you would come looking for me. Come, come," he said, taking me by the hand and guiding me past the imperious maître d'. I took one last look at the poor suckers who would probably still be sitting at the bar when we finished our brunch.

Once we were seated, I quickly glanced around at all the almost-famous faces. Plus the wanna-bes. The count was charming, as always.

The count decided to start things rolling. "So tell me about yourself, Robert," he said, staring into my face. His tan, chiseled face and the beautiful blond hair that topped his six-foot frame gave him a sophisticated, athletic look that suggested he spent winters skiing in the Alps, spring soaking up the sun in the piazza San Marco in Venice, and the rest of the year traveling from one fabulous location to another.

"Well, I . . ." I tried to say, but was interrupted by a very elegant-looking couple who came up to our table and introduced themselves.

"Count von Schmidt? It's Evelyn and Jim. Evelyn and Jim Brussard. We met you in the Hamptons two summers ago. At the opening for Joseph Deetherwill, the artist."

"Oh, yes! It is a pleasure to meet you again," the count said genuinely.

"If you're going to be in town for a while, we'd love to have you stop by for drinks sometime. Here's our card. We're still on Fifth," she reported, as if it were normal to live in some of the priciest real estate in the world.

"I don't know if my schedule will permit it, but if I have time, I will call you," the count replied, shaking their hands with the utmost grace.

The one thing I noticed through all this was that Evelyn and Jim didn't even acknowledge me. Not one bit. It wasn't that they didn't know me, it was that I wasn't a VIP or even a PYT (pretty young thing). It was me, my attire, my very presence. It just didn't say, "I'm extremely important and a linchpin of world culture and fashionable society." Instead, my demeanor shouted, "Born and raised in Michigan but escaped to New York—yet still from the Midwest, if you know what I mean."

It began to strike me that my slippery grasp of all things hip and with-it could be a problem in our relationship. The count and I came from very different worlds, and it showed in a lot of ways. And not just clothing. I had no idea how much fuel it took to fill a private Lear jet, when bluepoint oysters were in season, or whether riding sidesaddle was proper in Luxembourg.

When Binky and Biff left, the count spoke up.

"I have no idea who those people are. You see, I travel so

much and meet so many people, I have to be selective who it is I remember," he said, tapping his forehead. "I cannot remember them all, or I would be insane. These people, they all know me, but I cannot always return the recognition."

"Uneasy lies the head that wears the crown," I added.

"There must be no more of that kind of talk, Robert. You are my equal. All my life people are looking up to me because of my money or my social rank. I do not want to be aloof, distant. I want someone to love me, not my title. And that is why you are here with me. You believe in love. In its power. This is what I want from a man."

I was about to let the count know just how right he was when I noticed a man sitting at a nearby table reading a newspaper. In the middle of the paper were two small holes that the reader was obviously peering through to spy on us.

"Uh, Count, do you get followed a lot?"

"Whatever do you mean?"

"By the paparazzi?"

"I get my picture taken, but I am not Princess Caroline."

"Thank God! The last thing I need is another date with hairy arms and chronic man problems."

"Oh, Robert, you are so funny, too!"

"Thank you, Count, but we can get into that later. Back to the business at hand. Is there any other reason someone might be following you?" I said, gesturing discreetly toward the man behind the paper.

"I see. Well, we must get to the bottom of this," he said. He got up, walked over, and stood at the man's shoulder. "Ah, Michael. Why don't you come and join us?"

Michael put the paper down and looked up as if he were completely surprised that the count and I were there.

"What a surprise seeing you here, Count! And Robert, too!" Michael said with faux innocence.

I was about ready to order a drink, then throw it in Michael's face, but I realized it would take too long. After all, the service at F/E/2 was not only imperious, but agonizingly slow. I didn't bother to get up. Michael could hear me fine from where I sat.

"Ten thousand restaurants in New York, and I suppose it was pure coincidence you decided to come to F/E/2 for brunch the same morning we did?"

"You know how I'm drawn to trendy restaurants with bad food and lousy service," Michael justified to me and several nearby tables.

"Michael, you came here to spy on me and the count. Last night, you wanted to steal him away. Now you're following us. What's next? Will you be bugging my underwear?" I asked.

"No point in that. Not much happens in there."

"Well, having bugs in underwear is something you know a lot about. That's what the bulk of your dates leave you with."

"I haven't had lice in over a year, and you know that!" Michael said defensively.

The count, seeing that tempers were about to boil over, tried to intervene.

"No, Count, you don't have to smooth things over between Robert and me. I know when I'm not wanted." Michael stood up to go. As he began walking away, the tablecloth must have gotten caught in his belt buckle, because the entire contents of his table went right along with Michael. Well, only so far as to come crashing down on the floor in a hail of plates, glasses, and silverware. The noise seemed to shock even these egocentric diehards who never recognized anything happening in the world unless it was *their* world. Michael, head held high, walked out of F/E/2— tablecloth and all—into the street.

When Michael was out of sight, the count looked at me, waiting for me to say something. So I did.

"I'm so sorry about Michael. I know you can't afford to get tangled in scenes like that in public."

The count—er, Siegfreid—smiled at me, then reached across the table and took my hand in his. "I think it is very charming."

I was perplexed. "What, the catfight?"

"No, no. The way you fend off Michael when he clearly has designs on me."

"So you've noticed that already?" I asked, amazed at his perception.

"I could see it in the way he acted last night. He was crushed I did not fall for him."

I was desperate to figure out where he and I stood, so I went for it. "Did you fall for me, Siegfreid?"

"Absolutely. I am very interested in you. You are so simple, yet so complex."

"Yes, I've been told by several psychologists I have a complex. Mainly guilt."

"See, and there you go being funny again! So many things to like about you. Robert?" he asked, looking into my eyes—I think. It was difficult to tell with the ever present sunglasses. My clue was the way his head faced. It was like I was dating Helen Keller.

"Yes, Siegfreid?"

"I know it is perhaps very soon in our meeting each other, but I want to take you back to my hotel room and make love to you."

"I'm sorry, Siegfreid. I didn't quite hear what you said. It sounded like you said you wanted to take me back to your room and make love with me—but I know that couldn't be."

"No, I'm serious. Right now! I know it sounds, how do you say, pushy, but it just seems so right. Shall we go?"

My heart melted and, like Bob Dole getting his first prescription of Viagra, I felt what I hadn't in a long time: a hard-on.

2

My, What a Big Crown You Have!

Needless to say, we did go back to his expansive suite at the Pierre Hotel and we made mad, passionate love for three hours. It started tenderly and ended with such force we knocked over several large pieces of furniture in the process. It was the best I had ever experienced. Well, the only I had experienced lately.

He had food delivered to the room and we just stayed in and looked into each other's eyes—his green eyes staring intently into mine during a rare moment when he took his sunglasses off. On Sunday, it was more romance. We had a picnic in Central Park and went to the Museum of Modern Art, where Siegfried told me all about Kurt Schwitters and about the paintings of his he had in his collection. Then he took me out for an incredible dinner where we talked and talked. Then back to his suite for more lovemaking. When Monday morning rolled around, I thought I had reached the limit of my lovemaking. After all, Cinderella had to leave the ball while she could still walk. But a guy's gotta eat, so off to the advertising agency I went.

When I got there and opened the door to my windowless office (it had formerly been a telephone equipment room), a surprise greeted me. My office looked like Hillary Clinton's bedroom the day after the former first lady found out about

Monica Lewinsky's unorthodox ways of smoking a cigar with Bill. Orchids, roses, lilies—you name it—were there in every size, shape, and form.

Fellow workers gathered around my doorway, waiting to find out who my admirer was.

"A German count, if you must know!" I said, putting an end to their speculation.

They laughed and slowly drifted away, not realizing I had told the truth. See, even my coworkers didn't believe my budding romance (pun intended—never mind).

I gathered the cards from each bunch and arrangement and opened them one by one. They all said the same thing:

> *To the love that has bloomed between us. May I see you again?*
> *(And your stamen, too?)*
>   *Count Siegfreid von Schmidt*

Not only was the count in love, but in lust, too. I smiled at his bawdy joke, grateful for the fact that a count could be not only amorous, but randy.

I sat down and my heart began to race. It was really happening! Me, in love with a German count. I had to tell someone. Michael was out for obvious reasons. So I called my dear friend Monette, the lesbian who helped Michael and me beat a murder rap we were framed for a year ago in Provincetown.

"So spill the dirt! Are you a princess yet?"

"No, but I've been deflowered, then buried in them."

"So what was it like?"

"Monette! Isn't that kind of personal?"

"OK, if you don't want to tell me . . ." she said, setting the bait.

I waited only a millisecond before I bit. "It was wonderful!"

"You've got to tell me more than that! I haven't had sex

since New York was part of Gondwanaland, so I need to live vicariously through others."

"Shouldn't you choose a lesbian to live through?"

"What do you take me for? I don't need—or want—to know the number of thrusts per minute or the length of his glockenspiel. Just tell me about what it's like to make love to a count."

"Well, Monette, for starters, he wore his lederhosen and crown while we had sex."

"Kinky!"

"To tell you the truth, he's really good in bed. I mean, the best I've ever had."

"That's not saying much. Oh, Goddess, please don't take that the wrong way, Robert. You know I love you, but you have to realize our love lives have basically sucked."

"No harm taken. Anyway, gay men should take a lesson from this guy. He seems to be the only guy who understands the meaning of being passionate. He starts seducing you. Then he's very sensuous—with his hands, I mean. Rubbing them gently all over you. Tender, yet firm. Reassuring. Then he builds and builds, higher and higher, then backing off, then up again, yet higher this time. Then relenting a bit, then higher still. Hours flew by! Then he takes you to the top, and you've become this animal, I tell you. You've writhing and slithering all over the room, tearing it up in the process. It's the most romantic yet wild sex I've ever had, Monette!" There was silence on the other end of the phone, yet I could tell she was still there. "Monette? Monette?"

More silence. Then a few words managed to dribble out of Monette's mouth. "Go on, Robert. I think I just had an orgasm."

"You're just faking it! Did I tell you about the mink mittens he wore?"

"No kidding!"

"Yes, he put them on and ran them all over my body! It

was so refreshing to have a date use his hands to excite me and not to relieve me of my wallet."

"So what's next for you and the count? Marriage in Holland? White stag hunting in the Bavarian forest?"

"I don't know. We're just to the flowers stage. But, Monette, I'm really in love, I tell you!"

"That's fantastic! It couldn't have happened to a nicer guy. If anyone deserves it, you do."

"Thank you, Monette. That's the nicest thing you've ever said. I mean it."

"Well, I care for you, Robert. You've supported me through numerous breakups, including the last one."

"With the woman who wore feather-covered combat boots and brought a crow to work in a cage? How could I forget? I mean, she followed you around the city for weeks screaming *caw, caw* after you broke up with her."

"Your plan to get rid of her was brilliant," Monette admitted.

"I thought wearing that stuffed tiger tail out of the back of your pants and painting whiskers on your face would do the trick."

"I certainly appreciate your help with the Bird Woman. And I still have to thank you for bailing me out of jail for following Ellen DeGeneres too closely."

"That's what friends are for, Monette."

"Right. Now, don't take what I'm about to say the wrong way."

"Monette, give me a little credit."

"Good," Monette continued. "Have you ever wondered why the count would be interested in you?"

"Could you repeat that, Monette? I was distracted while withdrawing a knife from my back."

"You know what I mean. It seems a little far-fetched. I'm not trying to rain on your parade, but you need to be cautious. I don't want you to get hurt."

"You sound like he might be using me. Listen, Monette,

if he had some kind of fiendish plot up his Hugo Boss shirt-sleeve, I'm sure there are plenty of men in Germany he could use. Why come all the way to America?"

"I don't know, Robert. It just seems a little . . . not quite right."

"Monette, I don't know if he's really in love with me, but he makes a darned good attempt. But you haven't spent time with him like I have. I think maybe he's tired of all the fakery that comes with being a count and having money. Maybe it's like in *Roman Holiday* with Audrey Hepburn. He's tired of being a count and he wants a real down-to-earth guy like me who will love him for being a regular person."

"I still don't get it."

"You know, between you, Michael, my parents, and the Catholic church, it's a wonder I have any self-esteem left at all."

"I didn't know you had any to begin with."

"Well, I do, and as a matter of fact, it's one of the things the count loves about me."

"Your low self-esteem?"

"That's your interpretation. I prefer to call it my vulnerability. He says he wants to wrap his arms around me and protect me. Like a frightened bird."

"You're joking! That's nauseating!"

"Well, the way he said it, it sounded better. He put a little German accent on it and it sounded wonderful."

"I'm sure he could tell you to go stick your head into an orangutan and it would sound good to you. Well, take it easy and enjoy yourself. But be careful. Oh, and find out some more about him while you're at it. For my sake . . . and yours."

"The next time I see him, I'll grill him thoroughly."

"And when will that be?" Monette queried, letting me know her radar was up and trained on the count.

"Tonight. I hope."

I knew the wheels were turning in Monette's head. "Well, have a good time. And call me and report what you found."

"I will." As I hung up the phone, I wondered whether I should've told her about the fact that the count wore his sunglasses while having sex.

I spent the next few hours writing a brochure for a client whose overpriced and completely unnecessary home furnishings typified nouveau riche conspicuous consumption combined with new-age materialism. But at least these ridiculous items paid my bills. And it gave me something to work on besides the client to which I was regularly assigned—feminine hygiene products.

The Hemingway Clothes Hook *$34.95*

When Hemingway traveled to Africa for numerous safaris, he found the one thing he most missed about civilization was having a proper place to hang his pants. This beautiful hook is in homage to Hemingway and his very special need. Born in the same spirit of the African wilderness Hemingway once traveled, our hook is hand cast in brass and covered with several coats of hand-rubbed shellac to preserve its handsome burnish. The timeless styling will look perfect in any home decor.

It was a goddamned clothes hook made in Kenya for twenty-nine cents, then shipped to the United States, where an astronomical markup was applied, most likely to pay for the expensive stores that sold this stuff, their catalogs, and the people who wrote them. Yes, dear friends, this is what I did for a living—if you'd call it that.

Now you can imagine what went through my mind when I began to think about the count—a life of privilege I'd only dreamed about. The count flew on chartered private jets for the most part, didn't worry about the cost of a pair of really cool shoes, and didn't frantically try to reanimate dead house plants because he felt he couldn't afford replacements.

Of course, thinking about the life the count led naturally took me in the direction of thinking about the kind of life I *could* have with him. After all, it was very possible the count could present me with expensive gifts such as a Rolex Oyster Submariner wristwatch (the one with the black face and date/time and water-resistant to one hundred meters). I would have to learn to accept these tokens with grace, since to refuse them could cause insult to the count. After all, foreign customs are a tricky thing, and it's best to go with the flow in such matters. The count, being a generous soul, would no doubt not stop with a mere wristwatch. There would be clothes, trips to exotic locations, and maybe a Jackson Pollock for a Christmas present. Only one hundred eighty-six shopping days left!

The phone rang, jarring me from my daydream of instant riches. "Robert Willsop."

"This is Siegfreid. Did you get my gifts?"

"They're lovely. I liked your card, too."

"Since your office is so close to where I am, I would like to take you to lunch. I have a table reserved at Litmus at twelve-thirty. Can I expect you?" the count said, with just a hint of begging. This was too nice.

"Well, I was going to get a hot dog from a pushcart vendor on the street, but I guess Litmus will do." *This guy is unbelievable,* I thought. *He seems to know all the New York hot spots.* It was as if he read everything published about New York.

"Excellent! I will see you there at twelve-thirty," he said excitedly, then hung up.

I got the feeling he was going to spring a surprise on me at the restaurant. A gift, maybe? I had my hopes pinned on the Brandenburg gate, but I was afraid it might not fit in my studio apartment.

*   *   *

My intuition was right. When I arrived at Litmus, there was a beautifully wrapped package sitting on the table, just screaming for me to open it. As I sat down, I tried to remain nonchalant.

"For me! Siegfreid, you shouldn't have!" I said, feigning surprise. "And I didn't bring anything for you!"

The count was as charming as always. "You have brought me the most precious gift in the world. You."

"Oh gosh," I gushed, then realized I had sounded like a hayseed from Indiana. *Oh gosh?* I sounded like the kind of person who called his grandfather his grandpappy. Had I checked my overalls to make sure there was no manure on them before I sat down? I waited the obligatory three seconds before asking if I should open the gift now.

The count laughed. "No, Robert, it is an ancient German custom to buy an exquisite gift for someone, then not let them open it. Ever."

For a second, I believed him. He then chuckled and motioned to me to open the gift.

I began to tear at it like Morton Downey Jr. expecting a kilo of booger sugar inside, then caught myself. *Manners, Robert! Good breeding. Remember with whom you're dealing. Best not to be thought the greedy, ugly American.*

The paper gave way to reveal what was obviously an elaborate box containing a wristwatch with the most wondrous word in the world on top: Rolex. The box opened like a graceful scallop, revealing a gold watch, but not the Oyster Submariner. A flash of disappointment spread across my face, but I was able to hide my despair when I thought of the incredible sentiment behind the gift . . . and the comfort of knowing I could probably trade it in for the model I liked, with cash back to boot.

"Look on the back. I had it inscribed," the count said, beaming with pride.

In regal-looking lettering were the words that explained his intentions with no mistake:

Robert von Schmidt.
(Please make it so.)

I was so touched, a few errant tears escaped from my eyes. Then another thought went through my mind: I could forget about trying to trade it. (Why did I have this thought now? Jesus! One minute I'm Doris Day and the next I'm a ravenous gold digger hoping my rich husband has a bad heart. Care to go white-water rafting, dear?)

"Oh, Siegfreid, this is the most wonderful gift I've ever received!" I lied. The best gift I ever got was a motorized car park for my Matchbox miniature cars when I was nine. But times change.

"Will you become Robert von Schmidt?" he asked, looking into my eyes with such honesty and eagerness I was afraid that to say no would shatter him completely.

"You want me to take your name, Siegfreid? That's very serious."

"I am serious, Robert. I want you to go off and live with me . . . forever."

"Woah. This is so overwhelming, Siegfreid. Are you sure this isn't too soon? I mean, we have great times together . . ."

" . . . and sex," the count reminded me.

"Yes, that too. But you don't know a lot about me."

"So you are a murderer. Or an international art thief. I am still crazy about you."

"Siegfreid, I truly love you, but this is all so sudden."

"Please, Robert. You must come to Germany with me to live."

"Oh, I don't know, Siegfreid. The only German word I know is schmuck, which means penis."

"It does in Yiddish, but in German schmuck means jewels."

"See, I can't even speak German! There's so much to think about. I don't know."

"Robert, come away with me. I will show you the world."

"Siegfreid, I don't even have a passport. And my vaccinations aren't up to date. I don't think right now is such a good time. I'm afraid I can't."

"Robert, you must come away with me. I won't accept no for an answer."

"I don't know, Siegfreid. After all, I have a job to consider."

"Robert, come live with me, and you'll never have to work again."

"Never?"

"Never, Robert."

"When do we leave?"

3

Take a Walk on the Wild Side

After work, I met Siegfreid at his hotel and we made passionate love. We actually broke some more furniture in the process. For the first time in my life, I was living with wild abandon and I didn't care one bit. Of course, life is so much more carefree when someone else is picking up the tab, a fact to which Jane Fonda could no doubt attest.

We went out to dinner that night to celebrate my decision to become Mr. Robert von Schmidt. And, as usual, Siegfreid picked one of the hottest restaurants to go to: Desert.

We got a prime table immediately. Within seconds of sitting down, a bottle of champagne magically appeared.

"Siegfreid, this is wonderful! How thoughtful!" I exclaimed, looking at the label and noting the impressive name on it. Siegfreid raised his glass and proposed a toast.

"To Robert and your new life," he said, raising his glass.

I was just about to clink glasses with Siegfreid when I saw something that made my hand go numb. The glass slipped effortlessly through my hand, falling on the table with a loud crash. Right next to our table, Michael Stark was being seated with Marcus Leatherhill, the internationally famous male model.

Marcus was in every magazine and newspaper in New

York . . . and the world. Stunningly gorgeous, aloof, and completely unreachable, his square cheekbones and aquiline jaw were famous throughout the world. Fashion designers cowered in fear that he would turn down offers to be in their fall showings. Restaurants with questionable gastronomic output would become hip overnight if he graced their facilities with his presence. In fact, he once stopped in a seedy Bowery Street bar to make a phone call and the place became an instant hit. The other truth was that Marcus was haughty, imperious, and completely hateful, making him the most desirable gay man in New York. But no matter how you looked at it, there was no doubt about it: Michael was pulling out the big guns in order to get back at me.

I tried to mop up the champagne that had spilled all over the tablecloth, all the while casting an evil eye on Michael and his date. When Michael's ego suffered a bruising, he would stop at nothing in order to extract revenge. Typical narcissist.

Siegfreid deduced what Michael was up to and decided to let him know he was no fool. "Michael, another coincidence! We seem to bump into you so often," the count said, smiling graciously.

"Yes, it's really quite something. Nice to see you again, Siegfreid." He tried to omit me, then decided that it was too obvious. "And you too, Robert."

"Hello, Michael," I said.

"Robert, Siegfreid—this is Marcus Leatherhill. I'm *sure* you know who he is." Michael gestured to Marcus, who looked over at us briefly, nodded almost imperceptibly, then returned to his menu without so much as a single word.

Michael was so smug, I could've shot him right then and there. "Well, Count—and Robert—enjoy your meal," Michael added, feeling he'd had the last laugh.

I tried to return to my meal with the count, but Michael's overly extravagant gestures and forced laughter kept distracting me from my romantic meal. Michael had me just where he wanted me. I tried to make conversation with the count to tune out Michael's braying, which rose in volume at strategic times, like verbal karate chops to my ears.

"So, Count, thank you so much for the Lear jet for my birthday," I said, inventing imaginary gifts for an imaginary birthday. "And you were so lucky to get one in green, too! I heard Ted Turner had his eyes on that one!" Fight fire with fire, I decided.

Besides, Michael wouldn't remember that my birthday wasn't for a few more months. In fact, he never remembered, but made up for his abhorrent lack of concern for my birthday by snatching something from his apartment, tossing it into a shopping bag at the last moment, and presenting it to me as if he had battled anacondas in the Amazon to bring me the precious gift. The count played along.

"So you didn't care for the hunting lodge I gave you? It was bequeathed to my great-great-great-grandfather by the King of Prussia."

"Oh no, I loved it!" I said, gushing heavily. "It's so quaint!"

"Robert, I don't know how you can say that a schloss with thirty-seven rooms overlooking the Alps can be quaint."

Michael looked out of the corner of his eye, obviously hearing what the count had said, then raised his voice even higher. Anyone listening in on the conversation would've thought Marcus was stone-deaf. "So what did supermodel Naomi Campbell say when she looked over at Madonna and Angelica Huston, who were sitting next to Paloma Picasso, and fell over supermodel Kate Moss on the runway at the Donatella Versace fall collection in Milan?" Michael asked, successfully winning the world record for the most names dropped in a single sentence.

Michael thought his last utterance put him in the lead, but the count outmaneuvered him with a zinger.

"Robert, Tom Ford of Gucci has invited us to a small dinner party next week at his flat in Paris. Shall I RSVP?"

For Michael, it didn't get any better than Tom Ford. In fact, Michael had been trying to meet him for years—to no avail. When Tom Ford revamped the laughing-stock fashion label and made it chic again, Michael spent tens of thousands of dollars on an entire Gucci wardrobe, but still he was no closer to Tom than the pictures of him Michael collected and placed in a special leather-covered box he kept on his dresser. The count's last comment was stunning in its impact. It clearly raked the ramparts of Michael's fragile psyche of any remaining defenses. Michael was visibly shaken.

Then something even more extraordinary happened. Marcus, who looked as if he had been mulling something over for the last few minutes while Michael babbled incessantly, turned to the count and allowed several words to pass his hallowed, collagen-injected lips.

"Count Siegfreid von Schmidt?" he asked.

"Yes?" Siegfreid replied.

"I'm sorry I didn't recognize you at first," the supermodel decreed. "I heard Michael describe you as 'Siegfreid' at first, then I overheard this man . . ." he said, pointing to me as if I were an inanimate object.

"Robert! The name is Robert," I said, correcting Mr. Handsome.

"Oh, yes, Robert. I heard him call you 'Count.' It suddenly dawned on me who you were. I'm honored to finally meet you, Count von Schmidt. I've heard so much about you."

"All good, I hope," the count asked with the kind of self-effacing grace only a true royal could summon.

"Your palace in Berlin and art collection are unrivaled. I

would like to see them someday," Marcus admitted, making a discreet wink at the count.

The wink, however slight, wasn't slight enough to escape my attention. Or Michael's, either. In any other circumstance, the sly wink would have sent me to my battle stations. But in this case, it served to send Michael into a fit of jealousy that made his face redden, even through the Estée Lauder Night Repair Cream. I decided to do nothing. After all, Michael would be desperate now.

"I didn't realize you knew so much about me, Marcus. The next time you are in Germany, I would be happy to show you my collection," the count responded, returning a little wink of his own.

The count then turned and winked at me, too, letting me know his flirting with Marcus was nothing more than a well-deserved kick in the pants to Michael. The count began talking with me, only to be interrupted by Marcus again.

"Yes, Count, I would love to visit you . . . to see your collection, that is. I'm in Paris a great deal, and Berlin is just a short flight away."

"Please do that. Here is my card so you may call," the count said, handing his personal card to Marcus.

"Thank you, Count von Schmidt," Marcus said with a cunning smile. "I would like very much to take you up on your *offer.*"

The way Marcus pronounced the word, it dripped with so much sexual overtone that it needed a condom over it. I was really starting to enjoy this. Michael was squirming in his chair, glancing quickly at the count, then at Marcus, then me, only to repeat the cycle all over again. Clearly, he was overwhelmed and in full retreat. You could see the look on his face. It said: *Do something . . . fast.* So, Michael being Michael, did something fast. Which meant, of course, without thinking.

"Marcus, I think we've got to go. I think my spleen just burst," I overheard Michael say to Marcus.

"Your spleen? Are you sure?"

"Yes, I felt this pop," Michael said, pointing to his upper chest, "and I can feel something trickling inside of me. I'm sorry, but I've got to go to the hospital or something."

Marcus looked puzzled, but reluctantly got up from the table, along with Michael, who was now holding his lower right abdomen. At least he was getting closer.

The count and I stood up, showing mock concern to Michael, who waved us away with a don't-worry-about-me-even-if-it-turns-out-to-be-fatal-I'll-make-it-somehow look.

As soon as Michael had limped out of sight with Marcus, the count and I looked at each other, then burst into naughty laughter. Several minutes had passed before we could actually speak without starting another fit of laughter.

"Oh, my goodness," the count said, wiping a tear from his eye. "Your friend Michael never gives up, does he?"

"His ego would never allow it. But I'm not sure at this point whether he's trying to get back at you or me. Or both. With Michael, you never know," I consented.

"Well, the one thing I do know is that we need to start making plans for your future with me, starting with your job. Then maybe we'll go shopping for some clothes. You need a new trousseau."

"Could you have Gucci send me a complete wardrobe?" I asked.

"I can do better than that. I'll have Tom Ford whip up something for you. He's a personal friend of mine."

I was ecstatic! Not only would I be wearing some pretty fashionable duds soon, but I could rub the fact that I had met Tom Ford right in Michael's surgically altered face.

* * *

The next day, I went in several hours late and quit my job. When my supervisor asked if I was going to a rival firm, I said I wasn't. I merely told him I was going to become royalty.

When I called to tell my parents the news about quitting my job and maybe going to tour Germany for a while, I hoped my father would pick up the phone. No such luck. It was my mother, and she thought I had lost my mind.

"You can't *not* work!" my mother pleaded into the phone, ignoring the fact that trust-fund kids and Park Avenue trophy wives never raised a finger, except to accuse the maid of stealing. "Well, how can you go without working? Especially in New York, where the cost of living is so high? What are you going to *do* for money?"

From the tone in her voice, I knew just what she was thinking. Hmm. Son isn't going to work. Living in expensive city. He needs money. Where does money come from when you don't *work* in the traditional sense.

As usual, she was thinking the worst of things—and she was damned good at it. She was picturing me strolling down some garbage-laden street in Times Square in denim hot pants and a filthy rabbit-fur coat stolen from Macy's, trolling for toothless old men with twenty bucks to burn. Mom could take a completely innocuous event, pass it through her Catholic horror filter, and it would come out the other end nothing short of cataclysmic.

I knew how her mind worked. A television set left plugged in during a family vacation would burst into flames and consume our house while we were out having a good time. The lesson: don't have a good time. A stranger driving down her street too slowly was obviously studying her house, figuring out just how he would break in and steal her jewelry. The lesson: don't trust anyone. It's no wonder where I got my ability, as my therapist told me, to catastrophize. I learned from the best.

"Actually, Mom, I've got some money saved up and I thought I'd travel a little. I mean, I've never been overseas. Or anywhere, for that matter."

"What are you all of a sudden? Hemingway? What about your job when you get back from Germany?"

"Oh, they're a dime a dozen. I can pick up another one so easily," I said, hoping to put this matter to bed.

"You're not dipping into your retirement money, are you?" she asked, putting me on the spot again.

"No, Mom, I'm not raiding my 401(k) fund," I said in my defense.

"Well, if you have all this money, then why aren't you putting it into your retirement, instead of just gallivanting all over Europe and wasting it?" she said, blowing a hole right through me so cleanly, I almost didn't even feel it.

"Mom, this is what I'm going to do. OK?" I asked, as if she was going to agree with me. Fat chance. Under torture maybe, but probably not even then.

"Well, I for one don't know where your money is coming from, but I just hope you can pay your bills."

She was like the beast in one of those horror movies. After a terrific and bruising battle, you emerge triumphant over the prostrate beast, only to walk up to it and have its still-alive claw dart out and pierce you through the heart.

"Yes, Mom, I can pay my bills."

There it was in a horrible little nutshell: my mother's entire universe. You worked, you bought things, you paid bills, then eventually you died. The end. That was all life amounted to. Throw a monkey wrench into that perfect machinery and you had trouble.

I couldn't exactly tell her I was running away with a German count. In fact, I hadn't ever told either parent that

I was gay. Why bother? Like most parents, they knew—but they didn't want to know.

The conversation wandered into a standoff, with me eventually hanging up and wondering if pulling large hunks of hair out of my head for the next hour would be a productive use of my time.

4

How to Make a Sow's Ear Into a Sow's Ear Purse

The next day, I did the unthinkable. I picked up the phone and called Michael. Two things motivated me. First of all, his pathetic attempts to wrestle the count from my grasp had ended in disaster, with the count firmly by my side. So I no longer had to fear Michael's advances. Second, if I was going to become a member of the international jet set, I had to know how to act the part. If Michael couldn't teach this Midwestern Eliza Doolittle how to act and what to eat and wear, no one could.

"Hi, Michael, it's Robert," I chirped into the phone, hoping he'd be mature about a situation that was all his doing. After all, he was trying to steal my boyfriend.

"Robert who?" he replied, knowing full well who I was.

"Robert. Robert Willsop. Remember? I saved your life from those fag bashers years ago in the Village," I said, trying to wedge a little guilt into the situation. Nothing like reminding people they owe you their life to get them to see things your way.

"Oh, yes," Michael commented. "I seem to remember a friend by that name."

Michael was going to take the it's-all-your-fault route, so in order to get anywhere, I had to agree to be the bad guy—the story of my life. "Michael, I'm sorry about all the fuss between you and me. I guess I just wasn't thinking about your needs at the time," I replied, while biting my tongue and pinching the skin on my arm so hard it turned an angry red.

"Robert, you can't help being selfish. I mean, if I were severely out of shape, broke, and on the plain side and a count came along and wanted me, I'd have no qualms about muscling aside a dear, dear friend and dive for the count exactly the way you did. You have every right to be pigheaded," Michael said, turning the knife and rubbing salt into the wound at the same time.

"As always, Michael, you're absolutely right," I said, putting a silent curse on him at the same time. "So could you please forgive my shortsightedness? Can we go back to being friends?"

There was a long pause on the other end of the phone as Michael waited the requisite amount of seconds necessary to make me squirm in my guiltiness. Instead, I studied my fingernails.

Finally, the forgiveness and blessing came. "Robert, it's OK. I'll forget about your atrocious and juvenile behavior. Friends?"

"Yes, Michael. Now, I need your help."

"You've come to the right place. You see, most gay men don't really know how to give a proper blow job . . . " Michael began.

"Michael, that's not what I wanted your help on," I said, cutting him off.

"Why not? I'm the best."

"I'm sure half of the free world shares that sentiment, but what I need is for you to teach me how to be, you know, *with it.*"

"If you use phrases like 'with it,' you *do* need help."

"Michael, I need you to give me a crash course on being hip. You know, what to wear, where to eat, how to work out—how to live, really."

"Robert, I'm flattered you would ask me. Of course, you've again come to the right person. I like to think of my lifestyle as an art form and my life as a continuous work of art, with new masterstrokes constantly being added."

"Michael, that's funny. I've never looked at you or your life that way before. I always thought of you as nothing more than a rich slut."

"Robert, I know people who, for a price, can hurt you very badly."

"Sorry."

"That's all right. The city is full of thousands of jealous people who call me a slut all the time."

"Where do you want to start, Michael?"

"First we need to pump you full of steroids and get you into a gym so the count doesn't throw up when he sees you naked."

"Michael, I am not going to do steroids and become one of those overpumped freaks."

"Why not? I do them."

"Michael, they can cause terrible side effects."

"Dear, dear Robert. If you can't handle occasional rectal bleeding, recurrent diarrhea, shrunken testicles, and body odor that smells like an oily yak, then you're never going to have an incredible body like mine."

"Michael, no steroids."

"Fine, be paunchy. Maybe we can cover up things with a good haircut. I'll get you in to see Vladimir."

"Vladimir?" I asked.

"People call him Vladimir the Arrogant. He's *the* best hairdresser in New York. He does all the trendy people in the city."

I was beginning to have second thoughts about my plan to get hip and trendy. Could I handle it? Would I hate it? Was it worth it? Shouldn't I stay just the way I was?

"I'll swing by your place in about half an hour and pick

you up and we can start your makeover. Oh, that reminds me—I gotta run to the store and get plenty of food."

"I thought you always dined out."

"I do, but the cabala at my meditation temple got an e-mail from the spiritual leader, saying the world's polarity will suddenly reverse on Saturday and bring global chaos and cataclysmic weather changes. So we need to get your hair cut and weight training program started ASAP."

"You're joking."

"No, it's true. The e-mail said not to panic or tell anyone about it."

"So what are we mere mortals supposed to do?" I asked. If Michael's spending weren't so carefully watched by his tightfisted mother, I'd like to sell Michael some swampland in Florida.

"The e-mail said to get a lot of snacks to get through the crisis."

I couldn't believe Michael fell for this kind of stuff all the time. "So I can survive the coming apocalypse if I have enough Fritos on hand?"

"I guess so," Michael consented.

"OK, Michael. Do you think you can come down to earth for a few hours and meet me outside my apartment in half an hour?"

"Oh, yes, the shopping. Be sure and bring plenty of cash. Looking good doesn't come cheap."

"The count got a joint credit card for me. He says I can charge as much as I want."

"Perfect," replied Michael. "I'll see you soon."

I hung up the phone, called the count, and arranged to meet him for dinner that night. He said he had a lot of business to attend to and felt it was a good idea for me to spend some time with Michael.

Before I knew it, I was in a cab with Michael, heading toward the tony shopping enclave of upper Madison Avenue.

Michael pulled out a sheaf of paper and shuffled through

it, saying, "I've given the matter of bringing you into the twentieth century some thought."

"Not quite enough, Michael," I responded. "It's the twenty-first century."

"When did that happen?" Michael asked with a straight face. Obviously, someone had failed to brief him on this fact.

"A few years ago."

"Really? I guess I have to stop writing checks with the wrong year on them. Anyway, I've compiled a list of things we should focus on to get you to look like you actually live in New York."

"I *do* live in New York, Michael."

"Yes, but your clothes say Midwest. Your L.L. Bean wardrobe might be considered fashionable down on the farm in Iowa where you grew up . . ." Michael started.

"Michigan," I corrected him.

"Michigan, Iowa . . . does it matter?"

I was going to remind Michael that I thought Michigan was more progressive than Iowa, then realized he was probably right. There wasn't a lot of plausibility in crowing about the superiority of Detroit over Des Moines, so I chose to say nothing.

"I buy my clothes right here in New York. I'm sorry if they're not the latest thing."

"And there's another thing," he said, shaking a finger at me. "You're always apologizing for everything you do. Look at me. You never hear an apology coming out of my mouth."

"You can afford to act that way. You have money and you can get away with murder because of it."

"Robert, it doesn't take money. You just have to learn to stand up for yourself. Tonight, you and I are going to a seminar that would do you a world of good," he said, thrusting a pamphlet into my face.

"*Getting in Touch with Your Inner Asshole* is not something I'm in the mood for tonight. Or any night. Oh God, Michael! This is a seminar by that obnoxious asshole, George Baker. Why would you go to something like that?" I said, completely disgusted.

"It makes perfect sense to me. I know that *occasionally* I can be an asshole. I would think you'd be proud I admit to being an asshole. It's a big step in self-awareness."

"No seminar. Now, Michael—where are we going first?"

"Well, I thought our first stop should be to get you some glasses."

"My eyes are perfectly fine. I don't need glasses."

"Oh, Robert, no one is using glasses to *see* anymore. You're supposed to wear them to look smart."

"I *am* smart."

"There are some incredibly stupid people in New York and Los Angeles who have discovered they look smarter because they wear glasses they don't need. If they didn't wear a pair of some completely hip and trendy glasses, no one would take them seriously. I can't tell you how many people have confided in me that their careers took off once they got glasses."

Once again, I was stunned. "Michael, that's the stupidest thing I've ever heard."

"I bet you wouldn't say that if you had glasses," Michael replied, not realizing what he'd just said. But then again, he never did, including the time he stated that if Russia and the Soviet Union would just stop fighting, the world would be a much more peaceful place.

"Robert, how many times has your face graced the pages of *Vanity Fair* and *Details?*"

"None."

"And how many times have I been in there?" he asked.

"I have no idea."

"I'll tell you, because I keep count in a scrapbook. Exactly fifty-seven times as of this month. Now, do I know what I'm talking about?"

I had to admit, Michael knew what he was doing. Gallery openings, fashion shows, product launches—like a gay pig at a fashionable trough, Michael was there feeding voraciously. Like most people in attendance, he didn't give a damn about whatever event was being toasted. He just wanted to be there. And he was. To his credit, he did give generously. Being an heir apparent to a herpes-ointment fortune and having a family foundation behind him provided him with the deep pockets necessary to buy admiration in a city like New York. And fortunately for Michael, so many people were selling cheaply.

As the cab sailed down Madison Avenue, I began to wonder if I was doing the right thing. Was I pretending to be someone I was not? The count fell in love with me for what I was, and I feared that after a day with Michael, I wouldn't recognize myself. Like a fool, I voiced this concern to Michael.

"What do you mean you're afraid you might become a different person?" Michael said, with a mixture of puzzlement and horror. "I would think you'd welcome that opportunity with open arms. Now don't take this personally, but your life is dull and you're so tight assed, your butt probably squeaks when you take a dump! What I'm attempting to do is to make you into the sort of person everyone wants. You know, someone like me," Michael finished as we pulled up in front of the eyeglass store.

I relented. "OK, Michael, I'll go get eyeglasses."

The decision to ignore my better instincts and follow Michael's advice wasn't enough for Michael.

"And?"

"OK, I'll listen to everything you say from now on," I yielded.

"Good! You'll thank me for it."

We pulled up in front of the store on Madison Avenue and 65th Street, just high enough up from the tacky shops that now lined the once-fabled Fifth Avenue, yet not so high up Madison that it would disenfranchise the international set that clung to the East 50s.

The store not only intimidated passersby, but the doorman who stood guard on the sidewalk helped further convey the idea that only the foolishly rich should pass. In keeping with Michael's discovery that eyeglasses now indicated intelligence, the name of the store left nothing to chance: Eye-Q.

Once inside, we were pounced upon by our consultant, Celestine, who ushered us to a consultation booth (a desk to you and me) where she sat opposite us and stared intently not into my face, but Michael's.

I swear to God, this is what she said: "You look like you could really use some help. Don't worry, I'll get you a pair of glasses that will raise your visible IQ at least a hundred points."

Not bad, considering that with Michael, she was starting with negative numbers.

She continued, "What you have is an ovoid face with a square jaw line. It denotes strength, but to convey a higher sense of intellectual capacity, I'm thinking of frames that break up the vertical nature of your face and create a sense of stability."

Celestine was obviously unaware of the world around her, including the fact that Michael's natural good looks were anything but. His jaw had been deliberately broken and reconstructed, his dick implanted, his teeth capped, his lips injected, and his nipples "curtailed"—they were too large, he once told me. The expenditure was well worth it, I guess. Michael's dark, dyed hair, square jaw, and muscular body never failed to turn heads wherever he went. Michael was even the requisite male model height: six-feet-one. I suspected he was probably born shorter and had femur extensions added sometime during his teenage years.

"Excuse me, Celestine," Michael interrupted, "my friend Robert is the one who needs help."

"Oh," she said, letting fly the tiniest bat squeak of trepidation that perhaps with me, she had bitten off more than she could chew.

Michael attempted to distance himself from me, signaling to our face consultant that I was a friend, but not someone he would normally associate with. "Robert is going to marry this German count and he needs to be the hippest thing in Germany. I want every guy in Amsterdam and Berlin to think Robert is smart."

I didn't even bother to correct Michael that Amsterdam was in Holland, since it would lead to a protracted discussion of geography that would leave Michael insisting Brussels was a country.

"Why, isn't *that* a coincidence!" Celestine exclaimed. "We had a count in here this morning. He came in for some tinted contacts."

"What do you think the possibility is of that happening?" Michael asked.

"Almost never. I can't say we've ever had a count in here. Especially a German one," Celestine remarked.

I decided to take a shot in the dark. "Celestine, what was the name of this German count?"

"Uh, a Siegfreid von . . . Schmidt. Siegfreid von Schmidt," she reported happily.

"Wow," Michael jumped in. "That's the guy Robert is going to marry. Or live with, anyway."

"Well, he seemed like a real nice guy. Very intelligent. I could tell by the shape of his face. I couldn't see his eyes to discern his facial IQ because of the sunglasses."

"Yes, he says he's been wearing them for almost twenty years now."

"Well, you must be a very lucky guy," Celestine continued. "To have a rich, dashing lover who wants to sweep you off to Germany. Well," Celestine said, changing direction, "let's get you a pair of glasses that will have them drooling on the palace floor."

An hour and one thousand seven hundred dollars later, I walked out of the store with a pair of glasses I would never wear again, but would hold in reserve should I need to wow 'em in Berlin.

Our next stop was the Gucci store. I wanted to walk (and save the cab fare—why, in God's name, why?), but Michael insisted in taking a cab because "It's like twenty blocks, and besides, you can't be seen walking up to Gucci." Michael wanted to make sure every dime of money that could go into Tom Ford's pocket did. I guess Michael was hoping stories of his lavish spending would somehow get back to Tom, causing him to fall in love instantly with Michael.

The moment we walked in the door, the salespeople descended on Michael, figuring I was the ugly one with the money and the ability to buy the pretty boyfriend.

 Once the salespeople discovered I was the one to be fitted, they helped me buy armloads of clothes, all of them designed to make the wearer feel conspicuous and uncomfortable. After Gucci, it was off to Vladimir, where I was to get a haircut that would erase twenty-odd years of Midwestern plainness and vault me into the international limelight.

Vladimir, a hair burner of dubious Russian heritage, spoke for close to an hour explaining his theory of his plan of attack on my skull, sprinkled with bits of vicious gossip about people I've never heard of, then ran what seemed to be a chrome-plated miniature lawnmower over my skull in a matter of seconds that left no more than a quarter-inch burr all around my head. Thanks to Vladimir, I was about to embark for Germany and I looked like a skinhead. Too bad I didn't think of buying a hat at Gucci.

From Vladimir, we went for lunch at Café Vicuña, a contemptuous little restaurant on East 64th Street.

After leaving bag after bag of clothing at the front desk, we were ushered in and given a booth in a dark corner overlooking the entire dining room. This was Michael's favorite table, since it allowed him to watch everyone without being seen.

Michael ordered a fussy little salad and I followed suit. Then a realization struck me: I had carte blanche from the count, literally, so I stopped feeling guilty and ordered a bottle of champagne. I was celebrating, so why not?

As I looked around the room at all the elegantly dressed people wearing expensive jewelry, carrying unimaginably expensive handbags, and having hairstyles obviously not created by Vladimir, I began to realize how much I was beginning to like this new life of mine. In fact, I began to entertain feelings that I'd do just about anything to protect my lifestyle. Would I lie? Maybe a little white one now and then (oh, Count, no, I don't know what happened to your priceless Sevres porcelain clock that once belonged to Louis the XVI—I mean, why would you think I would be practicing my backhand indoors?) Would I steal? (Count, I just felt the gold bullion would be safer in my Swiss bank account.)

After all, Michael had pulled every stunt known to man in order to stoke the furnaces that powered his haute faggot lifestyle. This line of justification led me to consider the ultimate question: Would money turn a little boy from the Midwest into a calculating murderer?

For the first time in my life, I was glad my Catholic guilt kicked in. Murder? Me? Out of the question. Well . . .

I scanned the room again, and my eyes fell on none other than the count himself—with another man.

"Don't look now," Michael muttered out of the corner of his mouth, "but I think the count is pulling a fast one on you, Robert. He's sitting over there next to the flower arrangement with a good-looking guy."

Good-looking wasn't quite the word I would have used. Stunning was more like it. His suit was impeccable. His close-cropped, golden-blond hair (not dyed) and immaculately kept, pointy goatee were impeccable. Even his gestures and his posture seemed purposeful and calculated. Yet, in marked contrast was his rosy baby face, which made him seem natural and carefree. His demeanor said "trust me," but you sensed that this guy could be formidable.

"Yes, Michael, I see him. And why do you assume he's cheating on me all of a sudden? A gay man can have lunch with another man and it doesn't mean they're having an affair."

"Oh, yes it does! When I want to cheat on a boyfriend, I do lunch with my trick in case the boyfriend walks in and sees me. Then I can tell him I'm having lunch with a business partner. Let's go over and say hi so we can find out what the count is up to."

"Michael, please, don't go over there," I pleaded, grabbing onto his Gucci sport jacket so tightly, Michael gave me one of those don't-you-dare-put-a-crease-in-this-jacket looks. "I don't pry in the count's affairs—bad choice of words—personal business. I trust him and he trusts me."

"Robert, the reason he trusts you is because you couldn't bag a man if he were brought to you in chains. That reminds me, would you help me to remember to call Matt around three today? I have some *props* I want him to bring on our date tonight."

"Michael, do you really need all those toys in order to have sex?" I said, trying to set Michael straight, not that anything could—set him straight, that is.

"I usually add a toy here and there to spice things up. But I've really needed to pull out the big items lately. Ever since you started dating the count, my dates have gone from fantastic to the kind you used to have."

"That bad?" I inquired.

"It's almost as if you switched your karma with mine. Or you put a Polish curse on me!"

"Lithuanian, Michael. I'm Lithuanian."

"Well, I don't know what you did, but I have to get my sex life back on track."

"Do you ever think about anything besides sex?"

"Robert, you're always trying to point out things that make me look shallow and one-dimensional. I think about other things."

"Such as?"

"The economy," Michael retorted.

"The economy?" I asked, completely mystified.

"Well, buying things and my inheritance," he stated with complete sincerity. "And keeping up my looks. But can we get back to the count? If you want to stick your head in the sand and hide from the awful truth, we'll just sit here and watch the count and his friend for a while. But I'll lay odds that this guy is some kind of royal trick."

We ate our meal, but our attentions were focused on the count and his lunch partner. Michael was looking for any sign or clue that the count's intentions were anything but wholesome. Me too, but I didn't tell Michael that.

The count was obviously discussing something of great importance with his friend, since he looked straight at him the entire time, never letting himself be distracted by the passersby. Occasionally, he leaned toward his partner as if what he was saying couldn't be overheard.

"Sure looks suspicious to me," Michael interjected, trying to rattle the cage of my insecure mind. "If it's not some affair he's discussing, then it's probably some dirty family business thing."

"For a guy whose family owns controlling interest in a pharmaceutical concern, I wouldn't be flinging mud if I were you."

"Why, Stark Pharmaceuticals is one of the cleanest corporations I know. It's just that Mike Wallace from *60 Minutes* is trying to raise his career by dogging my family's business all the time. I mean, look, after the breast implant thing, we gave those women a lifetime supply of Wonder

Bras to make up for our product's failure. What more do they want?"

"Michael, you should run as the next Republican candidate for president. They need a callous and uncaring person to head the ticket, and I think you'd be just right."

"Let's get back to the count, could we please? Listen, I know I can seem self-centered at times," Michael said as I choked on my champagne, "but I feel very protective of you. And I think the count is having some pee-pee on the side."

"Pee-pee?" I queried, then decided it was better to let Michael's choice of words go unchallenged.

"Yes, pee-pee. You're too trusting of people. I don't trust any of my boyfriends any farther than I can toss them."

"I suppose you have a detective on retainer to follow them?" I surmised.

"Oh, God, no. It isn't the money. It's just that I don't keep any of my boyfriends long enough to get suspicious of them. Tell you what," Michael said, switching gears, "let me try something."

Before I could stop him, Michael whipped out his cellular phone and dialed.

"Yes, there is a Count Siegfreid von Schmidt lunching there at a table with a friend. Near the flower arrangement on the green pedestal. How do I know where the green pedestal is? I guessed. He's wearing a tasty little dark blue short-sleeved shirt from Hugo Boss with gray worsted wool slacks and square-toed shoes in black from Gucci, the ones with the buckles from last year's collection. Now, could you call the count to the phone and tell him to hold the line? I handle his finances in Germany and I'm doing a . . . ah . . . currency conversion, and we need him to hold the line while we do the calculations. We're wiring him a million dollars, and he wants to know how many Bismarks that converts to."

"Deutsche marks," I quietly corrected Michael.

"Sorry," he said into the phone. "It's a deutsche-mark-to-dollars kind of thing. You will call him to the phone? Good! Just in case I'm not on the phone when he answers, could you please tell him to hold? You will? *Danke, fräulein,*" Michael said, winking to me and giving me a thumbs-up signal, acting like he just fleeced some sultan out of a million dollars in diamonds with a single phone call.

I didn't like the sound of this. "Michael, what are you doing?"

"You'll see. Don't worry. He won't suspect a thing."

And with that, he got up and took a circuitous route through the restaurant, walked up to the count's table, and started talking to the count's lunching partner. I expected the worst.

Since Michael was immensely wealthy, he didn't just dish out attitude like other rich people. He shoveled. The rest of the population on this planet was here as a mere annoyance to Michael, wearing the trendy clothes he wore and consequently threw out when he saw commoners wearing them, making it difficult to get into trendy clubs without forcefully pushing, and constantly harping about the pollution caused by his family's pharmaceutical concern. When he walked around his apartment wearing a T-shirt that proudly proclaimed "It's all about me," he wasn't kidding.

Michael talked with the man at the count's table for a minute or two, then waved good-bye and left the restaurant. Moments later, our waiter came by with a note from Michael asking me to pay the bill and meet him outside the cafe.

I did as requested, fearing Michael was going to unload a dump truck of dirt on my romantic dreams and internationally famous life. As I walked up to Michael, I thought, *Oh well, it was a fun ride while it lasted.*

"You're not going to believe this. The guy says he's Uli, an art dealer from Germany, but he works through some gallery on Mercer Street in Soho."

I was elated, but flabbergasted. "Michael, did you ever stop to think for a second that he might really *be* an art dealer? After all, Siegfreid told me he was interested in picking up a few paintings."

"Robert, that is the first art dealer I've ever seen who wears a suit and looks like that. Or sounds like that! The guy had a ridiculous German accent."

"Michael, I forgot you're an expert when it comes to art dealers. Your last dealer tried to sell you an impressionist painting you later found out was done by a cat."

Michael rolled his eyes and let out a loud sigh. "OK, so I make one mistake and I never hear the end of it."

"*One* mistake? What about that guy who sold you those oversized canvasses that were painted by that artist who filled his butt with paint and then sprayed it? Ugh! Frederick Gombe. Some artist!"

"Well, Mr. Picasso, for your information, the artist soon died from toxic poisoning and his paintings skyrocketed in value. I made a killing on them."

I saw it was pointless to argue with Michael, so I relented to his constant prodding. "If it makes you feel better, I'll ask the count who it was when I have dinner with him tonight."

"Fine. If you want it that way," Michael said, carefully placing a thought bomb into my head and setting the timer.

As we walked to the curb to hail a cab, I began to wonder who the mystery man was. More importantly, I wondered whether I would have the courage to ask the count. You know, to be confrontational. As a Catholic-raised Midwestern boy brought up in a lily-white suburb, the answer to *that* question was painfully clear: nah.

I ditched Michael and lugged the dozens of bags of clothing, shoes, jackets, and accessories up to my shitty little apartment, aching to try everything on. So I did. Even though I harbored grave doubts about my ability to carry off the clothes I bought, I actually put them all on the floor and rolled naked in them.

When I regained my senses (or, more accurately, felt guilty about my lavish purchases), I called the count in order to meet him for dinner.

He suggested the Union Square Café, which was my favorite restaurant in the world. The food was not only fantastic all the time, but cellular phones were not allowed on the premises. This policy seemed to eliminate the technology junkies and Wall Street types, adding up to a restaurant that was civilized, quiet, and full of people who were appreciative of the food.

As I sat across the table from my soon-to-be husband, the thought kept running through my brain: had he been lunching with another lover?

"Well, Siegfried, how was your day?" I asked like a '50s housewife greeting her husband at the door to their modern-a-go-go cliffside house in Malibu dressed in Capri pants and a bare midriff blouse tied just below ample bosoms and holding a tray of martinis. (Don't ask me where that thought came from.)

"I paid a few visits on some old friends and went to Soho to check out the art scene. I saw a few interesting paintings by the late Frederick Gombe. They're a series entitled *Painted By An Asshole.*"

"I've heard all about them. I would have thought *Blow It Out Your Asshole* would have been a better title. Just be careful if you buy any of them, Siegfried, and wear rubber gloves before hanging them in your living room. So . . . you didn't do anything else today . . ." I said, like an interrogator trying to extract an confession out of a recalcitrant soldier with a barrage of pretty-pleases. "I mean, when you were hungry. I get so famished at lunch! I just *have* to eat. I imagine you do, too!"

The count looked like he was seriously doubting his command of the English language. He then proceeded, "Well, yes, I did have lunch."

I couldn't let him get away since I'd come this far. "So nothing out of the ordinary for lunch?"

"Now that you mention it, Robert, it was quite extraordinary," he reported.

My eyes lit up with anticipation.

"I had sautéed fiddlehead ferns for lunch. They were quite extraordinary. Oh, and a delicious wine from the Napa Valley."

"So that was it, just a plain ordinary lunch?" I asked, making a last-ditch effort to extract some kind of clue out of my cagey count.

"Yes. Why?" He looked at me strangely (duh!), making me feel guilty about mistrusting him and forcing me to abandon my line of questioning.

"Just wondering." Damn. I still didn't know where he had gone to lunch! I was reconsidering whether to just come out and ask where he had gone when he interrupted my plan.

"So, Robert, should we go out tonight and celebrate?"

"That would be wonderful! It would really take my mind off things."

So out we went. We had dinner at Casa Maraca, a fabulous restaurant where we saw a dozen movie stars and the bill came to over three hundred-eighty dollars. I felt like one of Michael's dates: I never even made an attempt to pull out my wallet.

Then it was off to the T Bar in Chelsea for drinks, then dancing at the ultra-hot Club Alta. I never had so much fun in all my life.

When the count finally let me off in front of my building at five A.M., it struck me how long it had been since I had stayed out so late. Years! And I actually let go of myself and just had fun. (Going out with Michael wasn't always the fun you would think; he often abandoned me for a hot date or treated me like a Tibetan sherpa, asking me to carry this or fetch that.)

As I approached my building in a fog of love, I failed to see the pile of dog doo left on the sidewalk and stepped right in it. But at that moment, something amazing happened. Instead of taking the offending footwear upstairs and scrubbing it clean while cursing copiously and loudly, I merely stepped out of my shoes and left four hundred fifty dollars of Gucci leather right there on the sidewalk—because I could afford to. Yes, folks, in the blink of an eye, I was now on a par with Michael Stark.

5

The Third Wives Club

That night, I had the weirdest dream.

I was walking through a huge palace. I came to an enormous set of doors and opened them. In the midst of the room was an elaborately carved bed with someone sleeping in it, the covers pulled up over their head.

When I pulled back the covers, the count was underneath, dressed like a Catholic cardinal. He shrieked at me and rose up out of the bed like a vampire and chased me with a huge crucifix. I ran and ran, but couldn't lose the irate count.

Eventually, I ran into a huge ballroom, and standing there in the middle of it was Russell Crowe dressed as a gladiator. Russell covered me with his brawny, muscular arm for protection and threw a spear at the count, causing the count to disappear in a puff of smoke. Russell and I then made passionate love.

I woke up just as Russell asked me to come to Rome with him to be his queen. I got up, opened a file cabinet, and pulled out a folder marked "health insurance." I immediately checked my deductible for psychiatric coverage, stared in horror at the co-pays, then decided calling Monette would be cheaper.

"Monette, I need your help."

"Now, why should I help you? I do believe you were the one who hired that drag queen to come to my office and deliver the three-foot-long dildo in a kid's red wagon two days ago."

"Me? You're accusing *me*?" I protested innocently.

"Don't play dumb with me, Robert. You were getting me back for having filled all those inflatable sex dolls with helium and tying them to the fire escape outside your apartment window. Not to mention the ones in the hall near your mailboxes, all of them addressed to your apartment and labeled 'rush delivery.' "

"So did Anna Rexia drag the wagon all the way down the hall to your office?"

"For all to see, Robert. I mean, people came running out of their offices. I liked the cute red ribbon tied around the dildo. Nice touch."

"God is in the details, Monette. Every time I think I've pulled the ultimate practical joke on you, you top mine. Escalation is inevitable. You know I can't let a challenge go unanswered."

"You'd better watch out. I'm planning my next joke on you with a man from the CIA who goes by the name of The Hyena. So what help did you need?"

"Just someone to talk to. I had the weirdest nightmare last night and it's bothering me."

"This isn't the one where your blind date comes to the door and you open it and you see Regis Philbin standing there with a bunch of carnations in his hand?"

"No, Monette. I haven't had that one since I stopped taking Prozac. Yesterday, Michael and I were having lunch at Café Vicuña and we spotted Siegfreid having lunch with another man."

"And?" Monette trailed off, wondering what the problem was with that.

"Well, he seemed to be talking like he didn't want to be overheard."

"And?"

"Like he was hiding something, Monette. I asked him about how his day was and he didn't mention lunch with his friend."

"And?"

"Monette, if you don't stop saying *and* and start feeding into my groundless paranoia, I'm going to start thinking you've got something against me."

"OK, Robert. Here's my guess. It's probably really far-fetched. Maybe he was lunching with a friend—an art dealer or someone—and he was throwing some big figures around and he didn't want those figures to be overheard. No, he didn't want to be vulgar, so he leaned in close to his friend so people didn't have to hear them discussing money."

"That's too logical, Monette. There's no conspiracy in your explanation."

"Fine, Robert. What really happened was he was meeting with a man named the Mongoose, a shadowy figure left from the collapse of the former Soviet Union, but now posing as a part-time annuity salesman. The waiter was actually an accomplice who was passing off the secret formula that makes Hello Kitty items so irresistibly adorable. The secret was hidden in a salmon filet, which the count ate and would later regurgitate, using vomiting techniques learned from New York supermodels. What's really happening is that the count is planning to flood the market with cheap Hello Kitty backpacks, thus plunging the circuit party accessories market into chaos. Plus, the count also knows your retina is identical to the president's and he's waiting to extract your eye some evening with a tablespoon, then fly it to Washington, D.C., so he can hold it up to a retina scanner and get his hands on the nation's most closely guarded secret: how Kim Basinger still manages to get decent movie roles."

"Monette, you're completely diabolical. And you're a cunt."

"Thank you, on both counts. Now, stop letting your

mind run away with you. Relax, for Goddess sake! You get so tight assed sometimes you could pick up a chair with your sphincter."

"Michael said the same thing to me lately, but not exactly in those terms. Your way sounds prettier . . . kind of."

"You know what I mean, Robert. I know this all seems too much out of a fairy tale to be believable. But so far, so good. And if it doesn't work out, you can always come back to New York and get a job the next day. I mean, the lousy jobs you've worked at are a dime a dozen."

"Wow, Monette! Thanks for making it all seem so hopeful and my life so meaningful!" I said, my voice dripping with mock glee. "Do you teach self-esteem-building classes on weekends?"

"Robert, was there a point to this phone call?"

"Well, just to tell you about the dream . . . and that I'm worried about whether the count is cheating on me with that art dealer."

"Oh, for crying out loud!" Monette pleaded into the phone. "What do I have to do to get you to put your insecure mind at rest?"

"Help me do a little snooping around on Siegfried's art dealer in Soho."

"Only if you promise me that if I help, you'll drop this whole art-dealer matter and find something else to obsess about."

"I promise, Monette," I replied, knowing Monette's assistance wouldn't put an end to this matter. The count could bring Uli to me naked and prove he was a eunuch, and I still wouldn't believe Siegfried.

"When do you want me to help you check out this Uli guy?"

"How about tonight after work?" I asked.

"Fine. I'll meet you at the corner of Mercer and Spring at five-thirty."

"Sounds great. I'll be wearing a trench coat with a red carnation on my right lapel."

"Until later," Monette said, about to hang up.

"Wait, Monette! There's one more thing: I also called to invite you to a bon voyage party a friend of Siegfreid's is throwing to celebrate our betrothal. Tomorrow night."

"Did you have any part in arranging this party?" Monette asked hesitantly.

"No, I didn't choose anything."

"Not even the music?"

"No."

"The food?"

"No, not even the food. I don't know anything about the party except that it's supposed to be kind of quiet," I said.

"When does it start?" Monette asked eagerly.

Later that day, I met Monette in Soho and we methodically went from gallery to gallery, asking if they worked with a dealer by the name of Uli. After hitting every gallery on Mercer Street, we found none had anyone on their staff named Uli. Worse, no one had even heard of him in the New York art scene.

As you can imagine, when Monette and I went to a bar afterward, I said nothing.

Monette, who knew me better than anyone I know, opened me like a book and began to read. "Let me guess. You think Siegfreid is a lying, two-timing megaslut who would have nonconsensual sex with a comatose, blind paraplegic just moments after having his way with an entire troop of Boy Scouts."

"Well, sort of," I conceded.

Monette continued. "Robert, just because Uli's story doesn't check out doesn't mean he's not who he says he is. Maybe Michael got his name wrong or mixed up the name of the street. You know Michael doesn't pay much attention to anything unless it directly affects him."

"I want to believe you, but I've tried and convicted Siegfreid in the court of my paranoia and he's as guilty as sin."

"I have a novel idea, Robert. Why don't you just *ask* Siegfreid about Uli?"

"C'mon, Monette! You're asking me to be mature about this whole matter? What do you take me for? I'd rather come up with cataclysmic and implausible scenarios that undermine my already slippery grip on reality."

"Suit yourself, Robert. Just give Siegfreid the benefit of the doubt for now. Unless you ask the count about Uli, you're going to drive yourself crazy . . . and I'm afraid that little foursome has teed off already."

"Thank you for your vote of confidence, Monette. OK, OK, I'll ask the count before we go to the party tomorrow night. How's that?"

"Fine," Monette replied. "There's just one more thing."

"What is it now?" I asked, exhausted by her line of questioning.

"I think my last sour-apple martini evaporated. Could you see what you could do about getting us another round?" she said, smiling.

I spent the next day puttering around my apartment, throwing out old magazines and organizing my closets. When the count came by early that evening, he entered. Without uttering a single word to say so much as, "I don't believe anyone could live in something so small!" or "My God, I've seen better places in East Germany just after the Wall fell," he pushed me backward toward the bed and made vigorous love with me before we left for the party. I know this fact isn't relevant to the story, but I feel the need to rub it in every chance I get, since it's a new thing for me.

I was going to pop the Uli question to Siegfreid in the cab on the way to the party, but I was in such bliss, I didn't have the heart—or the nerve—to doubt him. We arrived at a large loft in TriBeCa that looked like the manufacturer that formerly occupied the space had just moved out moments ago. It never failed to amaze me how lofts in this area could charge such high rents and still look like parts of downtown Beirut.

The elevator ground dubiously upward, leaving us on the top floor with signs pointing down the hall to a large loft. The door was wide open and the room was completely silent.

The moment I entered with the count, dozens of people jumped up and shouted *surprise* with such volume I almost soiled my underwear.

The loft was almost raw, but it was wondrous. The walls were painted blinding white and the space was filled with a few sofas scattered here and there. But the best part were the dozens of metallic pillows filled with helium that floated around and around, pushed into flight by large electric fans. It was straight out of Andy Warhol's factory. The only sour note was sounded by a huge banner strung across one wall that proclaimed, "Bon voyage, Robert. Belgium, here you come!"

Michael no doubt had had a hand in the decorating.

I tried to make out some familiar faces in the crowd, but I didn't seem to recognize anyone. Just then, Michael elbowed his way to the front of the crowd, planting air-kisses on the count and myself with all the sincerity of Elizabeth Dole welcoming a member of the North America Man/Boy Love Association into an all-boys prep school.

"Did I surprise you?" Michael asked excitedly.

"Absolutely, Michael. I had no idea."

"Well, the count was in on it. He gave me a list of his friends."

"Michael?" I asked, still looking in vain for a recognizable face. "I don't see any of *my* friends. Are they here yet?"

"Well, Robert, most of your friends suck and are more boring than insurance, so I invited a lot of my friends. I hope you don't mind. I mean, you want this party to be fun, don't you?"

I quickly calculated how much it would cost to have Michael killed—or at least have all his white spandex circuit party wardrobe slashed to pieces—and wondered how I would ask the count for the money.

I looked around and quickly saw all the signs of Michael's friends: people who looked like they hadn't worked a day in their lives, partied all night, and didn't have two nickels to rub together.

One of the partiers, dressed in black and wearing a sport jacket that looked like it was spawned by an unholy coupling between a hausfrau cotton dress and a furry car coat, strode toward us. He was also wearing a red leather neck brace studded by metal insignias that presumably signaled a new trend I wouldn't be following.

"Siegfreid, my darling!" our fashion victim gushed, throwing his arms around the count and giving him a big, mushy kiss.

"Robert, I'd like to you meet Elmore, one of my best friends this side of the Atlantic," he said, gesturing with pride toward Elmore.

"Glad to meet you Elmore," I returned. No sooner had I said, "The count has told me so much about you," that I realized that the count hadn't really. I mean, I had some sketchy details, but nothing much.

At just that moment, Monette came up to me, took one look at Elmore, shook her head as if trying to reset her brain, then did a double take at Elmore, figuring she really was seeing what she was seeing.

"Excuse me, Siegfreid, Elmore, but I'd like to introduce my good friend, Monette."

Monette extended her hand. "Monette, this is Elmore. And this . . . is Siegfreid."

Monette's face lit up, and she shook hands with the count. "Well, thank you for inviting me here. Robert has done nothing but talk about you and," she said, smiling in that devious way of hers, letting me know she was going to drop a bombshell, "the furniture you've broken."

Normally, I would've strangled her right then and there with the dream catcher (lesbian catcher) that hung from her car's rearview mirror, but I was actually proud of my sexual accomplishments. Before the count, my idea of wild sex meant I would leave my socks on.

Introductions were made all around and drinks were promptly fetched by waiters who looked like they were hired away from a Communist airline, their serving skills still intact from training that equally emphasized serving in-flight drinks and garroting capitalist spies with movie head-phones.

Monette pulled me aside, asking me if I had questioned Siegfreid about Uli.

"He came to my apartment and had his way with me," I whispered. "How was I supposed to ask him after that? It would sound like I don't trust him."

"You don't," Monette reminded me. "You think he's cheating on you."

"Well, it sure looks like he is. To tell you the truth, I don't think this guy's name is Uli and I think he made up the whole art dealer thing."

"But think about it, Robert. You said neither the count nor Uli saw you in the restaurant. So if they had no reason to think anyone was watching them, why would this guy make up this fake name and story about his being an art dealer? It doesn't make any sense."

"I don't know, Monette. I just can't help but be suspicious. It's my nature. Just look at Siegfreid's friends," I said motioning to the people at the party. "They all look so unreal!"

The count's friends seemed to be of a much better class than Michael's—big surprise! They seemed to be witty, intelligent, well-mannered, and were vastly different from the people who usually attended the parties I was invited to. No, the parties to which I was usually invited were populated by people who threw up on your shoes, had sex in the bathroom, or stole things. Michael's parties differed only in that his revelers dispensed with the bathroom and had sex right in full view of everyone else. It was nice to step up in class from the trailer-trash crowd I was used to.

The count spotted someone else and pulled him toward Monette and me in order to make an introduction.

"Robert, Monette, I want you to meet another friend of mine. This is Uli Steben, my art dealer. Uli, this is Robert and Monette."

It was none other than the man Michael and I saw having lunch with Siegfreid at Café Vicuña. He was still stunning and impeccably dressed. I felt like such a fool to have suspected that the count was cheating on me.

"It is a pleasure to meet you, Robert and Monette," Uli said, extending a hand to shake.

Monette shot me an *I told you so* glance. Like I didn't feel stupid enough already.

"Well, I guess that settles that," Monette commented to me out loud, knowing only she and I would know what she was talking about. "Siegfreid, would you excuse us for a moment? I have something to discuss with Robert."

"No, no, not at all," the count replied, then dived back into the crowd with Uli.

When Monette and I were out of earshot of anyone we knew, Monette turned to me and said, "Well, I guess that puts the final nail in the coffin of your cheating theory. Now forget about this whole matter and go have fun with the count."

"You're right. When you look at it, my life couldn't be better. I have an honest-to-goodness German count who's head over heels about me, I'm about to leave for Berlin and live in the lap of luxury, and I will probably never have to work again. Try and top that, anyone."

When I thought about how my luck had turned around practically overnight and looked nowhere but up, I realized I had no right to be anything but enormously happy. And I was! I was flying on a cloud until I overheard, not one, but several guests ask one another, "So which one is the count?"

I was ready to dismiss these party-crasher comments when I heard one person say something even more obnoxious: "So which one is the count and where's the gold digger who's sunk his hooks into him?"

I was just about to scratch the offender's eyes out when I was distracted by a waiter who happened to drop an entire tray of canapés on my pants.

The count came running over to me, wiping fruitlessly at my pants in order to make it look as if I hadn't rolled across Wolfgang Puck's kitchen counter. I looked over at Monette, thinking this was one of her practical jokes, and shot her a glance that accused her fully.

"Now, Robert. Who do you think I am? An amateur? Paying a waiter to spill food on you is child's play," she responded.

"Poor Robert," the count said, dabbing some more. "There, it doesn't look so bad! Just a little cheese in your cuffs. The dry cleaner will get that out in no time," he said, rising to a standing position. He pulled my head downward and planted a kiss on my forehead, and I swear it made me feel better.

"Maybe I'd better go to the bathroom and run a little water on this," I reported, thinking it would probably be better if I tried to make a composed reentrance—minus food.

"Robert, we'll cut the cake after you clean yourself up. So hurry back!"

I headed off to the bathroom, which I found to be decrepit and almost unusable. Was living in TriBeCa worth this? Of course, I couldn't throw a stone of condemnation very far myself. My studio apartment more closely resembled a heroin-soaked, fifth-floor walkup from a 1970s drug-smuggling movie than a presentable habitat for someone paying in excess of one thousand four-hundred dollars a month—and I was lucky to be paying that.

I was about to reach for the water faucet when, from behind the shower curtain, came the very faint sounds of breathing. I slowly parted the curtain with my finger and saw two men who were obviously very happy to see each other.

"Michael, could you come outside soon? They're going to cut the cake," I said, flinging the curtain open and exposing them completely—what little wasn't already exposed.

I walked out into the hallway and passed a scary-looking woman dressed in military fatigues who walked into the bathroom, saw Michael and his instant date, and proceeded to use the facilities without so much as a thought about her audience of two.

"In the Israeli army, we go to the toilet side by side, we are all equal," the woman said, as if that made everything all right.

"When you gotta go, you gotta go," I responded.

I was making my way to the bar for another martini when the count swooped down and collected me.

"It's time to cut your bon voyage cake! Come this way! And I have arranged special entertainment for you!" he said proudly.

Siegfreid made an announcement that the festivities were about to begin and everyone crowded around, making me feel even more self-conscious. The inscription on the cake was in German, so the count translated for me.

"It says 'Good fortune and a good life, Robert!'" the count announced to all. "Now blow out the candles!"

I made an attempt at blowing them out, but could tell from the suspicious sparking that the candle flames produced, the count was using those relighting joke candles that were impossible to blow out. It was clear the count felt I had never seen such a thing and was proud of the fact he thought he had pulled a fast one on me, so I didn't have the heart to tell him this joke was older than Goldie Hawn.

"It was Monette's idea to use the joke candles," the count confessed.

When Monette played practical jokes, she followed a certain pattern I had been able to discern over time. Her jokes usually came in threes, with each succeeding joke more devastating than the last. One down, two more to go. There was no letting my guard down now.

I cut the cake and passed it around. Michael emerged from the bathroom just in time to get a piece.

"Michael," I said, handing him a plate, "here's your piece . . . not that you didn't just get one in the bathroom a few minutes ago."

Michael smiled. "I'm sorry about that, Robert, but I've been after this guy for so long. You know, the funniest thing is he said he was attracted to you, but I said you were taken, so I figured he was fair game."

"So was he fair?" I asked.

"He was great!"

"Did you get his phone number?" I asked, trying not to show too much interest.

"Yeah, but I flushed it down the toilet. I tell these guys I'll call, but I never do."

I decided to put all my cards on the table. "Did you ever think I might want to contact him just in case this thing with the count doesn't work out?"

"No. Robert, your problem is that you hold on to the glimmer of a distant hope too much. What you fail to realize is there's always another guy standing in line waiting. Just move on, is what I say."

"Just eat your cake, Michael. Oh, and another thing. I just met the guy Siegfreid was having lunch with at Vicuña the other day. Uli *is* an art dealer. So there."

Michael looked at me as if I had just showed him a certificate entitling me to a portion of the Brooklyn Bridge.

"Who told you this?" he said, scrunching up his eyes in disbelief.

"Siegfreid just introduced me to him."

Just when the world was starting to make sense, Michael pulled the rug from under my feet and my tidy, ordered world where everything is good and sensible came tumbling down like a house of cards.

"My God, Robert. Do you believe everything people tell you?" he said, firing another mortar shell into the ruins of my world.

"What do you mean? The count just introduced me to Uli and told me point-blank Uli is his art dealer!"

"Look, I know you're a little naive at these things, being from Ohio and all," Michael began lecturing me.

"Michigan, Michael. I'm from Michigan," I said, setting the record straight.

"For God's sake, Robert! I wouldn't say that so loud if I were you. People are going to know you drove the family combine to your high school prom!"

"For your information, I drove my mother's Pontiac Bonneville to the prom."

"That's just as bad. Maybe worse. Say, who let you into Manhattan? Didn't the border guards stop you at the tunnel?"

"Yes, the fashion police pulled me over on the New Jersey side, but I made a break for it and swam the Hudson River instead. But to get back to the story, Michael, you were just about to belittle me and destroy my confidence by telling me how naive I am."

"Oh, yes," Michael said, recomposing his thoughts and

reloading his cannons. "Uli—if that's his real name—is definitely having an affair with the count. He knows we're on to him, so he puts Uli right out in front to make it look like he's got nothing to hide. It's like hiding an object in plain sight."

While I wasn't quite sure Michael's twisted logic explained the situation, he seemed so sure and matter of fact that I believed him. My line of thinking, however, was interrupted by the count, who stood up on a chair and clapped his hands to get everyone's attention. "I have some entertainment for you now, so if you will all take your seats, we will begin!"

Siegfreid motioned to a chair in the center of the front row, where I would have a bird's-eye view of the proceedings. The lights in the loft dimmed, and out from the kitchen strode several men in traditional German folk costumes, complete with Tyrolean hats and lederhosen and carrying accordions, glockenspiels, and tubas. They played several tunes and actually got the jaded New York audience to start clapping to the music.

When they finished, a piece of opera music came on, and as the music built to a peak, a huge drag queen dressed up as Brunhild appeared and galloped back and forth in front of us, her wired gold braids dancing in tune to the music.

But that wasn't the only thing that danced back and forth. Her breasts, as big as watermelons, twirled and swirled to a beat of their own as she hurtled herself across the stage. No mere amateur, this drag queen had fashioned realistic but false arms on her costume, while her real hands were hidden in her ample bosom. This allowed her breasts to do the sort of acrobatics available to only the most physically coordinated chesty girls.

Brunhild then dashed up to me, surrounded my head with her breasts, and pounded on my head to the music. For a person who raised feeling self-conscious to an art form, this was one of the most exquisite forms of torture Monette could play on me. To her credit, she was doing a damned good job. Two jokes and counting.

Brunhild skipped away from me like a demented Heidi of the Alps, picked up a wooden picnic basket, and started tossing flowers out into the audience. When she had exhausted her supply of Alpine ammunition, she looked at the audience in mock surprise as if she had found something in the bottom of her basket. She tiptoed up to me, reached in the basket, and hit me smack in the face with a pie. On tasting it, however, it turned out to be apple strudel.

Monette would pay dearly for this one.

The guests erupted in gales of laughter, and someone snapped several pictures of me in my moment of glory. I decided to be a good sport and stood and bowed to the audience, all the while plotting revenge on Monette. The count, laughing hysterically, handed me a towel he had hidden underneath his chair for the occasion.

"Oh, my goodness, Robert. I hope you don't mind, but Monette thought this would be a good way to send you off to Europe. I was worried at first that this joke might have gone too far, but you have taken it like a man," he chuckled. "Let me go get you another towel," he said, setting out in search of something to clean me off.

Monette appeared at my side, martinis in hand, and offered one to me. "I think you could use one of these," she said.

"Thanks. You know this means war."

"Yes, yes, I know. But how are you going to get back at me from six thousand miles away?"

"I don't know that yet, but believe me, I will find a way."

"Oh, Robert, guess what? A very attractive woman here gave me her business card. I might give her a call."

"If she's a friend of Michael's, I'd run the other way."

"No, no, she says she's a friend of the count," Monette reported, burying the card in her wallet.

"That's wonderful, Monette. It can't hurt,"

The count showed up holding a large towel, which I used to wipe the excess strudel off my clothing.

"Siegfreid, could we go? I'm getting tired and it's been a long day."

"Fine, fine, we can leave right now," he said, putting his arm around me.

The count's tenderness and concern made me forget the fact that Siegfreid might have a lover on the side—for now, at least. The three of us walked out of that party, arms around each other, feeling that the whole world was in love that night, Siegfreid, Monette, and me. Not to mention the "kick me!" sign Monette had taped to my back while I wasn't looking.

The next few days were filled with packing and getting my crummy apartment ready for the deep slumber it was about to undergo. As much as I loved the count and felt that this relationship was the one, a tiny voice inside my head told me to hold on to my chilling little apartment for a while. The count, astonishingly, agreed, telling me it would give me the feeling of a safety net and would put my mind at ease.

I gave plants away, had mail forwarded to Germany, and cancelled magazine subscriptions. I cried slightly when I locked the door to my studio and walked downstairs to the waiting limo that would take me to the airport.

Monette was down in front of the building, fighting back tears. I was, too, the moment I saw her.

"Now, now, we look like we've just come home from one of our dates!" Monette said, trying to interject some humor into the situation. "Let's not look at this as meaning we're not going to see each other anymore. Let's think of it as a way for me to visit you frequently . . . at your expense," she said, winking at the count. The count smiled back, not truly realizing he would indeed be paying for her flight. As Monette often said, her salary from the Endangered Herbs Society of America, where she worked, barely got her back across the river to Brooklyn each evening.

Monette looked at me, gave me one of the sternum-cracking hugs only a six-foot-four lesbian could give, and told me to watch out for myself. I was just about to get into the limo when a taxi screamed to a halt, blocking the limo's path. One of the doors flew open and out popped Michael, out of breath and with a gift in hand.

"Had sex with the driver, I see?" I said, figuring what I said was not only intended to be humorous, but was also completely plausible.

"Sorry I'm late, but this guy from last night just wouldn't leave!" he said, his words coming out in big puffs of air. "Here," he said, shoving the gift into my hand. "Something to remind you of me, because I know you're going to miss me."

Blow, oh winds of self-aggrandizement, blow!

"Thank you, Michael. You are my reason for living," I said in a sarcastic reply that was lost on Michael.

"You know, Robert, you're not the first person who's told me that!"

"Uh, Michael, we've got a plane to catch, so take care of yourself and always remember to rinse your mouth after you spit it out." I got into the limo and it whisked me out into the streets of New York and toward my new life.

As the limo sliced its way up Third Avenue, the count looked down at the gift in my hand, then up at me.

"Aren't you going to open it?" he asked. "It seems like Michael went to a lot of trouble to get you this gift in time. It must be very special to him."

I tore the wrapping paper off the gift (which showed un-mistakable signs of being hastily wrapped) and opened the box inside. I was not prepared for what I found: a paperweight in the shape of a tube of herpes ointment obviously given out free to doctors by salesmen from Stark Pharmaceuticals. Attached to the tube was a frantically scrawled note from Michael that read: *"Good luck in Germany, Robert. I hope you never need this."*

6

Ich Bin Ein Berliner . . . Sort of

The flight was positively luxurious. No screaming kids kicking the back of my seat, no waiting in lines for the bathroom only to pee on yourself because of the close quarters, and no shitty meals cooked in Peoria, then flash frozen and reheated in microwave ovens. No, siree. Even though the count didn't personally own this plane, only leased it, it lacked none of the comforts of home. (Gee, I wish my home looked like this.)

We dined on braised shank of veal with pureed carrots and sucked down champagne until I was literally flying. As I looked down at the little people below me, I noticed the count staring into my eyes with far more than an I-love-you look. The look said I-want-you-now.

Without a word, he lifted my hand and gently coaxed me by the arm into the bathroom. I don't want to go into intimate details, but for the next hour, the two of us became members of the mile-high club. When we finally emerged from the bathroom, I was drenched in sweat. As I tried to walk nonchalantly down the aisle of the plane, the steward gave me a sly wink and pointed discretely to my Gucci shoes. Stuck to the bottom of my left shoe was a used condom that clung there like Jackie Collins to a Revlon makeup counter. I wiped my foot in a macho way on the carpet and kicked the offending piece of latex under a seat, pretending this sort of thing happened all the time.

The count, who saw the entire episode, didn't seem to care one bit, owing to the fact he probably got away with more than the average person. What struck me more and more as I really got to know the count was how much sleaziness lurked underneath his civilized and royal exterior. His sexual urges seemed insatiable—not that I was complaining. I guess I never fathomed the vast differences in the private and public lives of celebrities. I mean, look at the cool, calm, and collected faces you see at the Academy Awards. I'll bet plenty of those actors know more about rubber cat suits than they care to let on.

I drifted off to sleep and dreamed of walking through the palatial rooms of the Schmidt estates that were so big the count and I needed Roller Blades in order just to go to the bathroom in the middle of the night. I slept on beds of rose petals and ate roasted hummingbirds with silver forks that required a muscled and naked stud to lift to my lips— not because of the weight of the silver, but because I couldn't be inconvenienced. I was just about to ask one of the men in livery (with the crotches missing and their buttocks exposed) to go fetch a pistol because I wanted to shoot at some of the fine Sevres porcelain that lined the walls of the room, since I had the reputation of being madcap and carefree when . . .

. . . the count lightly shook me awake.

"Robert, we're beginning the descent into the Berlin airport. Did you have a good nap?"

"Yes. Yes, I did. I was dreaming about Berlin."

"About the great sex we will have in all the rooms of my houses?" the count asked, reading my mind so completely, I felt naked and exposed—not a bad place to be where the count was concerned.

"Oh God, no," I said, lying through my teeth. "I was dreaming about . . . the colorful flower carts on the street corners in Berlin."

"Robert, those disappeared forty years ago," the count said matter-of-factly. "And believe it or not, we even have electricity and television."

"Oh," I said, feeling I would never make it in Germany. After all, it had taken me years to adapt to New York. I still let people walk all over me for fear that if I spoke up, someone would pull out a gun and shoot me. Even cranky old ladies that a two-year-old could beat up shoved their way in front of me in grocery store lines.

The plane circled over ugly buildings then touched down, the bump of the wheels making it clear there was no going back—easily. The count looked over at me and said something I thought was truly touching.

"Robert, because I am quite well known in Germany and somewhat in Europe, many people make many demands on my time. But I want to keep you all to myself. I want to be selfish with you. So can you understand I want to limit the time I spend with friends here in Germany and spend it all with you?"

I didn't know what to say, but I managed to eventually find a few words. "Of course, Siegfreid, I understand. I see how everyone in Europe would want me," I said with a wry smile.

The count got my joke and smiled back. "Good! As far as the world is concerned, there is just you and me," the count said, extending his hand to shake on the deal. We shook, then kissed.

The plane taxied around to a private gate, the door opened, and I walked into my new life. We were standing in line for customs when they asked to me to open my suitcase. I did as the official requested, only to find something I didn't recall packing back in New York: a dildo the size of a fire hydrant. Our agent's face said, *What are you going to do with this, scale it?*

The count was watching the entire ordeal and began to laugh hysterically, something I rarely saw him do.

I quickly reached one conclusion and decided to check it out.

"Monette put you up to this, didn't she?" I asked, knowing full well the answer.

"She said it would be her parting gift to you."

"Well, I'll get her back for this one. Even if I have to reach across the ocean to do it," I said, closing my suitcase when the agent was finished.

The agent, whose name tag said R. Reimann, looked at my passport, then waved me on. When he looked at the count's passport, he asked Siegfreid to remove his glasses so he could see his face completely. The agent stared at the count, then at his passport picture, then back at the count. I imagine the agent didn't know what to do about the count. Since Siegfreid changed his appearance so often, I can't imagine how he could even remotely resemble his passport picture. For that matter, who did? My picture looked like I had spent the night being beaten in a third-world prison for opium smuggling.

The agent excused himself for a second, taking the passport with him and disappearing beyond a door with an official seal on it.

I was getting worried, but the count showed no sign— even beneath his sunglasses. Me, I was worried stiff. What if the count was a cocaine smuggler kingpin and I the unwitting mule, the secret lining in my suitcase stuffed to the gills with cocaine?

Shortly, R. Reimann returned and excused the confusion with an explanation in German. The count translated it and told me the agent was concerned that he didn't look like the person photographed on the passport. "Happens all the time," he said, chuckling. The customs inspector asked the count to open his suitcase. R. Reimann pawed carefully through the clothes, stopping now and then as if he had found something illegal, then surprised me and signaled that Siegfreid could pass.

A chauffeur greeted us on the other side of customs and scampered to carry our bags and escort us to an imposing Mercedes sedan with deeply tinted windows. I got in and, for some reason, began thinking of Princess Diana and her last voyage through that tunnel in Paris. Safety first, I thought, pulling my seat belt so tight it almost sliced through my waist. Luckily, as the car sped away into the city, I spotted no paparazzi chasing us. We had no sooner left the airport when Siegfreid pulled out a cellular phone and placed a call. I couldn't understand his German, but I did manage to understand the words Karl and Helmut. Seeing my curiosity, he hung up, then turned to me to explain.

"The servants. I want them to meet you when you arrive at the house. I want you to feel, how do you say, comfortable. They are there to make you feel at home."

I nodded eagerly, acknowledging his thoughtfulness.

The suburbs eventually gave way to the tree-lined streets of Berlin, and lower-class neighborhoods gave way to better ones. As we entered what Siegfreid said was the Charlottenburg section of Berlin, the car pulled through a gate and up to an enormous town house mansion that looked like it was centuries old, yet its neighbors seemed far newer.

"How old is your house?" I inquired.

"It was rebuilt shortly after the war. It was completely destroyed, but my family rebuilt it from the rubble. It looks well, don't you think?"

"It looks, well, big," I said, trying to get the whole of it within my scope of vision. The building stood back from the street and was surrounded by a wall topped by a tall and menacing iron fence. While the wall said "keep out," the heavy iron gate that protected the circular drive in front of the house stood wide open. The house certainly wasn't large enough to be called a palace, but I resolved to refer to it by that name, regardless. I was going to live in a palace, and no one was going to contradict me.

A man I assumed was a butler greeted us at the car, speaking German to the count and motioning to us to go inside. We did. When we entered the house, I was met by a hastily assembled all-male staff whom stood beaming at me. Siegfreid introduced me to each member of the staff.

"Robert, this is Karl, my manservant. He will help you with anything you need. He lives here with us, in a wing at the back of the house."

Karl was all smiles as he shook my hand limply. Karl was what I would call a German circuit boy, about thirty-four or thirty-five years old, the perfect height of six feet, and strikingly handsome, with blond hair cut short, a tanned complexion, and eyes so blue they almost blazed in his face. Finishing off his perfect face was a pair of glasses identical to the ones that Michael had cajoled me into buying back in New York. Not that I was ever going to wear mine, but seeing them on Karl's face meant I could never don them in his presence.

"Karl also speaks a fair amount of English," the count added.

He pulled me to the next person in line.

"Robert, this is Helmut. He is our wonderful cook and is here only during the day. You will find him mostly in the kitchen or around the coolers in the second basement. He will make you whatever you like, so please let him know if you need anything special."

Helmut smiled and shook my hand. He was gorgeous, too, but more striking than circuit-boy gorgeous. His shaved head and Vandyke beard accentuated his sharp and distinctive face, a face so focused and lacking in anything superfluous, it perfectly reflected the German penchant for technological precision.

The count then gestured to seven men in line and described their role at the house. I would have guessed they were high-priced call boys, but I constrained myself long enough to hear the count's explanation.

"This is Herman, and he and his six helpers come in once a week to keep this big house clean. They are very good, and I am very happy to have them here," he said, invoking smiles from the entire Berlin clean team. "The gardeners are not here today, but you don't need to be concerned with them. They know what to do and they do it very well, I must say. Anyway, thank you all for assembling here, you are dismissed," he finished. For those who only spoke German, he repeated his dismissal to them and they all filtered back to their respective places in the enormous house.

If perfect Karl and gorgeous Helmut hadn't made me feel like a skanky whore, Herman and his cleaning crew did the trick. I knew for a fact Siegfreid had chosen me over these men, but I couldn't help but wonder that if these guys were so good looking, what were they doing here? The answer seemed obvious: to get at the count and his money. I resolved to put the idea out of my head. After all, Siegfreid hadn't looked at any of them with lust in his eyes. In fact, he hardly even noticed them. OK, I told myself, end of matter, case closed. For now.

Siegfreid put his arm around me and started leading me down a hallway, presumably beginning a tour of his palace. The more he showed me, the more I knew I was in love . . . with the count, of course. The house wasn't bad, either. I expected cluttered interiors filled with Louis de Hooey furniture, but was pleasantly surprised to find a mix of ancient antiques and cutting-edge modernism.

The count toured me through a dozen or so rooms until I said I had lost my bearings. The bedroom was beyond anything I could imagine. It had a vaulted ceiling painted exquisitely with fat little cherubs and likenesses of gods.

"Remarkable," I said, truly meaning it.

It was amazing, but upon closer inspection, it was even more out of the ordinary. The gods (no goddesses on this ceiling, baby) depicted not only had schlongs (mental note to myself: learn the German word for "dick") that were grossly out of proportion to their bodies, like mythical Billy dolls, but they were doing very ungodlike things to each other. I don't want to get into great detail about all of this, because being from the Midwest it embarrasses me, but I don't think the ancient Greeks or Romans had leather slings and their cherubs didn't hover near the gods offering cans of Crisco. The only thing I could think of at that moment was, who did you call when you needed something like this painted? A twisted skinhead artist named Otto?

As I lowered my gaze from the ceiling and laid eyes on the grinning count and the way something in his trousers said *achtung*, it was clear I was about to see Berlin from a different perspective: on my back. The experience was not only enjoyable, it also gave me a better insight into how Michael Stark saw the world.

The count wasn't kidding when he said he wanted to keep me all to himself. The rest of my first day in Berlin and most of the night was spent in wild passion. At around four A.M., Siegfreid finally left me alone long enough for me to drift off to sleep. Later that morning, I got a huge surprise.

I awoke when I heard Siegfreid enter the bedroom carrying a huge breakfast tray containing a huge silver dish with domed cover. He could see the curiosity in my eyes and lifted the dome to reveal the contents: a tiny present wrapped with a red bow.

"Open it, my little cherub."

I opened the present and inside was little more than a key—a key with the Mercedes three-pointed star logo attached to a sophisticated-looking remote control that looked like it could open the doors of a car on Venus from Earth.

"What's this, Siegfreid?" I asked, knowing all too well the answer to my question.

"Go over to the window and see!" Siegfreid said excitedly.

Since the windows of his bedroom overlooked the front of the house, I got up and went over to take a look. In the driveway was a black Mercedes sports car the likes of which I had never seen before—or probably will again. It looked like it could drop bombs on Iraq without showing up on radar.

I turned from the window, stunned. Stunned that anyone would give me a present that didn't have an electric cord and a ninety-day manufacturer's guarantee attached to it, and stunned that I was now officially a gay gigolo (the Rolex watch didn't count—you become a gigolo once you receive a gift costing more than ten thousand dollars).

"Oh my God, Siegfreid . . . "

"God had nothing to do with it," Siegfreid replied. "A wedding present."

"A wedding present? Aren't you a little premature? I mean, Germany is more progressive than the U.S., but is gay marriage legal here?"

"No, but it is in Amsterdam. That's where we are going to go soon. We will be married there. And, no tears allowed . . . *ist verboten*, OK?" Siegfreid said in response to the fact that I was about to get all mushy. "Now, here is perhaps the most precious gift of all," he said, pulling out a gorgeous legal-sized envelope made of the most beautiful handmade paper I have ever laid eyes on.

I opened it and found a legal document inside. I tried to make sense of it, but to no avail.

"I will translate it. It is my will and it says that if I should die, everything I have will go to you. Everything."

I heard ringing in my ears and surmised that this was what a stroke felt like. I couldn't believe it. I stood holding the signed and notarized document like it was one of Jesus' original coloring books. Wow!

I felt an overwhelming sense of the possibilities before me. It was beginning to look like I was set for life. The count obviously wanted to keep me on, with marriage just weeks away. Plus, if he should suffer an untimely death, I would be wealthier than . . . Michael. Hmm.

I pictured myself as the consummate femme fatale, or German black widow, so to speak. I would be toasted and feared at the same time by the hippest people in the world. The whispers I heard behind my back hinted I had killed the count to get my hands on his money. And they would be right, but the smile I constantly wore behind my widow's veil would say, *You'll never prove it*. Men would be irresistibly drawn to me because of the danger I exuded and the mysterious air that surrounded me. I would . . .

. . . just then, the count seemed to be shaking me awake.

"Robert! Robert! Are you OK?" he said, concerned I had indeed suffered a stroke.

"Oh, gosh, no, Siegfried. It was just so . . . overwhelming! I'm fine."

"Well, if you are feeling good, then let's take your new car for a ride, yes?"

"I guess so," I answered.

We went for a ride that I have to describe as the most exciting in my life. The hushed interiors, the concert-hall sound system, and the engine that hummed in that way only a German-engineered car could, all made the trip unforgettable. My favorite part was when we pulled out onto the autobahn and Siegfried told me to push the accelerator down to the floor. The car seemed to lift up off the road and lurch into space. Trees and houses went whizzing by in a blur of light. When I told the count I almost had an orgasm, he saw to it that I did—right there in the car. Never mind the other drivers on the road.

As we flew down the road, I have never felt more reckless in my life—or more alive.

What was becoming of me? Where was the neurotic, prudish Midwestern boy who comparison-shopped toothpaste, routinely apologized for things he never did, and wouldn't think of turning the dial on his stereo beyond the forty-decibel point? I must have left him back in the United States.

Good riddance. He could stay there for all I cared.

After my "auto-erotic" experience, we came back to the house for more sex that ran late into the night. Not that I was complaining, but I began wondering if there was more to our relationship than sex. I certainly was no Michael Stark. I couldn't be happy in a noogie-only relationship. I needed shopping, fine dining, and great clothes, too.

I woke up the next day and found myself alone in the sumptuous bed with Porthault sheets (I looked at the label—who wouldn't?). I stared around the room and pinched myself for my daily morning reality check. Nope, this was still real. I got another dose of reality when the count kicked open the door, bearing a large tray filled with an exquisite breakfast.

"Siegfreid, I have a question to ask you, and I want you to be honest."

"Yes, dear Robert. What is it?"

"Are you real?" I said bluntly.

The count hesitated as if he didn't understand my question, looked horrified for a second, then replied, "Why ever would you ask a thing like that?"

"It just seems that this is all out of some fairy tale."

"Well, Robert," he said, finally smiling, "you've seen the Internet and the gay magazines. I *am* a fairy, you know!"

"I guess that would explain it. Are you the maid, too? I mean, I thought a count didn't lift things."

"Well, I will tell you something right here now. You have a saying in America that good help is hard to find. Well, imagine yourself in a socialistic country where no one wants to work, especially now that the Wall has come down. It's not these people's fault. They never learned how to work. But no one in Berlin wants to work anymore. So, consequently, I have many servants that stay only a few days or weeks, then leave. Or they steal things from me. It is a big problem! I can't seem to keep help very long. I am very happy to have Karl and Helmut. But I never know how long they will stay with me. It is not that I am a bad man, for you see I am a very nice person, don't you think?"

"Siegfreid, you seem like the nicest person in the world. Like you're magical," I said.

"Well, I do have a magic wand," he said.

"I've seen it. It *is* magical," I admitted.

"No, not that one, Robert. But I do appreciate the compliment you pay me. No, I am talking about this magic wand," he said, brandishing a fork and waving it around and around my head, "and I am going to wave it and later this week, you and I will fly to Monte Carlo. Poof! It is done."

"Oh, Siegfreid, that sounds too wonderful!"

"Good. It is a long time since I've been gambling. And, Robert, you must see the hills overlooking Monte Carlo. Maybe we can take a drive up in them and have lunch outdoors."

Just as the count finished his sentence, I heard what I guessed was a doorbell. I didn't know that palaces had doorbells, but my suspicion was confirmed when Karl came to the bedroom door, knocked, and reported to the count that someone wanted to see him.

"Who is it, Karl?" the count asked, with just a hint of irritation in his voice.

"He says it is urgent business," Karl responded.

"Did he tell you his name?" the count asked.

"No, but he said you will know him."

The count left me in bed and went downstairs to receive his visitor.

I finished the last of the coffee in the coffeepot on my tray and decided I could use another cup. After all, I was the boyfriend of a count. I could have anything I wanted. I put on the wonderfully soft waffle-patterned robe left lying on the bed for me and walked downstairs. I was heading toward the kitchen when I heard Siegfried's voice coming from a room down the hall. It was a voice that was not pleased, because I could hear a few outbursts, then quiet.

I was just about to make a turn and go into the kitchen when the door to the room opened. A man left the room and made his way down the hall toward me, then turned to go out the front door. The man, who was dressed in jeans and a T-shirt and didn't look like the kind of acquaintance the count would make, was smiling as he departed.

The man was definitely familiar. It wasn't Uli, the count's art dealer. All I could think of when I looked at the man was "glasses." I don't know what that meant.

Siegfried then came out of the room, banged the door shut behind him, saw me, and froze.

"Robert! There you are! Looking for something?" he exclaimed.

"The kitchen . . . I need some more coffee."

"Yes, let us get you some more. You must have everything you desire," he said, giving me a great big kiss and then grabbing my arm and escorting me down the hall.

"Siegfried, is everything all right? I mean, I heard you raise your voice, so I was worried something might be wrong."

"Wrong?"

"I don't know. Your businesses or something," I said, supplying the answer.

"Oh yes, that! A messenger from one of my companies. He has come to tell me one of our ships has run aground! Somewhere in the North Sea! See what I told you about the difficulty of finding good help?"

"I hope not oil!"

"No, not oil, Robert. Too early to tell what was on board. Oh, well. I guess some earl at Lloyd's of London will be going without a new Ferrari next year," the count said, chuckling to himself. "Never mind about these things. I did not bring you here so you could worry about my business. We must instead think of Mad Queen Ludwig's party here in Berlin. It is the most important—and how do you say, ex-clusive—gay party in Europe."

"Mad Queen Ludwig?" I asked, not sure that I wanted to hear the answer to my question.

"His name is Ludwig Buxtehude. Everyone calls him Mad Queen Ludwig because of his ancestor and because he is a drag queen and wears the most fabulous dresses, espe-cially at his ball. Only a few hundred people in the world will be invited to his masquerade party."

"Uh, Count?"

"Yes, what is it, Robert?"

"Do you think I can invite Monette to the party? I miss her."

"Yes, Robert. Whatever you wish, it is granted because Ludwig and I are friends. What about Michael? Do you not want to invite him, too?"

"He's on vacation. I called him the other day. His an-swering machine didn't say where."

"Fine. Call Monette. Invite her here to Germany. And tell her to bring a fantastic costume for Mad Queen Lud-wig's masquerade ball!"

I went to the phone and called Monette.

"Monette? It's me, Robert."

"Robert? Oh my goddess! Why haven't you called me? I missed you!"

"I've been so busy, Monette. Beating the servants, hunting wild boars, you know . . . royal stuff."

"Wearing out those knee pads I gave you is more like it."

"You mean the ones with the flag of Germany embroidered on them?" I asked. "I found them in my luggage, along with a piece of latex that will go unidentified."

"Robert, I have no idea what you're talking about."

Monette was six thousand miles away, yet I could see her smirking on the other end of the telephone.

"Don't worry, Monette. I'll get you back. Plus, now I've got the financial resources to carry off a practical joke of the kind you can only dream about. You have been warned. Look, I miss you and want you to hop on a plane in two weeks and get your ass over here to Berlin. I need someone to talk to, and you're invited to the most exclusive party in Europe."

"Which party is that?"

"Mad Queen Ludwig's," I said as if it were natural to attend parties with names like this.

"Mad . . . never mind. I won't ask," Monette answered.

"I just want you here. It will make me very happy, and the count wants me to be happy," I said proudly.

"I'll bet you've been making the count plenty happy already."

"Well, I have to admit I have been paying particular attention to one crowned head of Europe."

"My goodness, how we've changed! Before the count, you never spoke to me about sex unless you used your little Midwestern euphemisms."

"What Midwestern euphemisms?" I inquired.

"Like 'naked leapfrog' for fucking. Or 'pulling the freighter into the dock.' "

"Well, you'll see how much I've changed when you get here."

"Robert, you've only been gone a few days. You know it takes a lifetime to get over the dysfunctional backgrounds we come from."

"It takes electroshock and a croquet mallet. That's what my former therapist used. So ask for time off at work and start packing your bags. I'll send you the airline tickets and your itinerary. First class, of course. Oh, and find something really fantastic to wear to the party. It's a masquerade ball."

"Robert, in case you've never noticed, I'm a six-foot-four lesbian who has never worn a dress in her life. Where am I going to get something fabulous?"

"Why don't you call what's-her-name? You know, the lesbian who does costumes for the Met opera?"

"Lynette's her name. Good idea, Robert. I'm sure she can whip up something in two weeks."

"Fine, Monette. Siegfreid and I are heading out to Monte Carlo in a few days for a quick honeymoon."

"Whoa! Very well done, my little boy toy!" Monette snickered with a dirty tone in her voice. "The only place my dates take me to is the Olive Garden."

"Have fun and we'll see you the day of the party here in Berlin. We're getting back that morning."

"Bye. Watch out for the count's one-armed bandit when you're hitting the sheets in Monte Carlo," Monette said, then hung up.

I smiled to myself, then picked up the phone and called my travel agent in New York. After arranging for Monette's flight, I placed a call to Lynette.

This was going to be good.

7

From Lady of Leisure to Lady of the Evening

Siegfreid said he had some business to attend to that afternoon, so he gave me a fistful of deutsche marks, a walking map, and told me to go out on the town and enjoy myself. So I did.

Even though I could afford to take a cab, I decided to walk, since that would eliminate the possibility of getting into a language stalemate with a shady cabdriver who didn't speak English and decided to take me to my destination by way of Czechoslovakia. I was glad I did, because it gave me a chance to see how Berliners lived. I have never been so excited in all my life. I was amazed at the energy of the people as they whooshed by in their minuscule cars or dashed down the street. Their clothing seemed to be years ahead of even New York. And everywhere you looked, there were cranes sprouting from practically every block, transforming this former Cold War city into the glittering new capital of Germany.

I went into a KaDeWe department store and had a splendid lunch, complete with several glasses of German beer, then attacked the local shops, buying several pairs of shoes I felt were guaranteed to turn Michael Stark green with envy.

I got back to the palace around four P.M., only to find Siegfreid hadn't returned yet. I went to a room filled with books and started reading the only book I brought with me from the United States, Stephen Hawking's *A Brief History of Time*. Had Michael seen me reading this title, he would've taken one look at the jacket photo and pronounced me a nerd. And he would be right.

I got up and tossed the book into the trash, thinking that cosmic physics wasn't something a count's lover should be reading. So I picked up the latest issue of *Stern*, determined to learn who was who in Germany. I didn't know if I was going to like being shallow. It took too much work.

As I was reading, the door opened, and in walked Karl, holding a vase of exquisite white lilies.

"Many excuzes, Herr Willsop! I am very mooch zorry! I deed not know you are here!" he apologized profusely and in very broken English.

"It is good, for I am quiet and you did not know, Karl," I said, sounding like Yoda in *Star Wars*. Jesus! How was talking like this supposed to help Karl when I hardly understood what I just said? "So, Karl," I started, trying to strike up a little conversation, "do you enjoy working for Siegfreid?"

"He is very nice, but I do not know him . . . long. I only verk for him a leettle time."

"Oh, yes, Karl. Siegfreid told me you just started with him. Helmut, too."

"Yes, both of us are new. Yah, I like verking for Herr Schmidt, but dere is so much verk to do!"

"Yes, it seems like much work for just two people! But I imagine the cleaning people help out?" I asked, concerned that, as a trophy wife, the least I could do was to run a tight ship for the count.

"Oh yah, dey make my job mooch easier. But dere is much for me to do all the time. Herr Schmidt had many more people to help not long ago."

"Yes, Karl. He told me it is difficult to get people who work well."

"Dey verk for him long time, then he kick dem out."

This news sent a tiny little signal of discomfort through my suspicious brain, but I felt I needed to have all the facts before I judged the way Siegfreid ruled his household. I was sure getting good help wasn't easy. He had told me so himself.

"I am zorry, Herr Willsop, but I haf many tings to do. I vant you to haf a pleasant day," he said, his voice trailing off so low I almost couldn't hear the rest of his sentence. He left the room, politely closing the door behind him.

It occurred to me I might still be experiencing a little jet lag, but I'd swear to God that Karl had just called me a *verthless whore* before he wandered away.

The count came back to the house around seven P.M. He found me in the kitchen having a glass of champagne with Helmut, who was busy preparing a dinner of penne with fresh cherry tomatoes, Kalamata olives, and goat cheese as I watched. I wasn't completely comfortable being left alone with Karl, so I gravitated toward the man who seemed like the least threat. Plus, Helmut had never called me a verthless whore. At least, not yet, but the day wasn't over.

"Siegfreid," I said excitedly, "I bought something today I thought you would get a kick out of."

"You bought something? Well, I must see it!" he replied, trying to match my enthusiasm word for word.

I left the kitchen and ran upstairs to our bedroom. Since I couldn't remember what shopping bag the item was in, I carried the lot of them downstairs and back into the kitchen. As I pushed the door open, I caught Helmut with his arm practically around the count, showing Siegfreid how to garnish the top of the penne on each plate. I say caught, because it looked quite suspicious to me, but since Helmut didn't jump back or withdraw his arm hastily, he lent the entire incident an air of innocence. I tried to be open-minded about the whole thing. I had been in Europe only two days, so I figured perhaps Helmut was living up to the European reputation of people standing close to each other when they talked. After all, I couldn't expect others to respect my idea of personal space. If that were true, I would be at ease only if Helmut were standing in Belgium.

While I was uneasy about what I discovered, I felt better when I saw Siegfreid thought nothing of Helmut's closeness. It was as if the servants in Siegfreid's life practiced gay chokeholds on him all the time.

I pawed nervously through several bags and found what I was looking for.

"Let us see what you have there," Siegfreid said as he casually pulled away from Helmut and examined my purchase. When he didn't burst out laughing at my gift, I felt the need to explain it.

"It's a Mister Hanky stuffed toy. From *South Park*, a television program. He's a talking piece of poop. Squeeze him," I said, encouraging Siegfreid to join in the fun. He did as I asked him and Mister Hanky rewarded us with a rousing "Hai-de-ho!" salutation from his hidden voice box.

No laughs from either the count or Helmut. Just puzzlement.

I continued to dig my grave deeper. "He says other things, too ... this one speaks in German, no less! Mr. Hanky is very popular in the States!"

No guffaws. Not even a knee slap.

"It's not as funny if you're sober," I said, tossing the disappointing toy onto a counter behind me. It was time to change the subject. "Are we ready to eat?"

"Yah, it's time," Helmut reported, carrying our dishes out to the dining room. Siegfreid and I sat down while Helmut returned with a bottle of Italian white wine from the kitchen. He gently eased the cork out of the bottle, which came out faster than Helmut expected and flew to the floor along with the corkscrew.

"I am most sorry, Count," Helmut apologized, then bent over to retrieve the cork, holding his position just long enough to offer his snugly clothed butt for Siegfreid to admire. I stared in shock at Helmut's stunt, but Siegfreid either didn't notice or chose to ignore it. Was I going mad, or was all this really happening right in front of my nose?

Helmut picked up the cork and put it in his pocket. He poured the wine, checked the table to make sure we had everything we needed, and withdrew to the kitchen. I was going to say something, but I was in too much shock. Any moment now, I knew I was going to wake up and find this was all a dream and I was still in my crummy apartment in New York, still worked in a dead-end job, and had no boyfriend.

To prove that this was all a dream, I stabbed a fork into my hand and . . . winced from the pain. Nope. No dream.

I merely smiled, dug into my salad, and wondered what the hell was going on in this house.

"How did work go today?" I asked the count, trying to introduce some sort of normalcy into the evening. It wouldn't hurt if I knew a little bit about where Siegfreid spent most of the day, either.

"Oh, much of the same. Ships coming in, ships going out. So many details."

Siegfreid's answer told me about as much as I knew about him to date, which was zilch.

"And how was your day, Robert?" he asked. "Did you have a nice time shopping and seeing Berlin?"

"Yes, I enjoyed everything—except for this woman."

"A woman?"

"Yes, on the street. She started yelling at me. She kept yelling 'oinky staff' and pointing at me."

"Are you sure she didn't say *die Einkaufstasche*?"

"How did you know? Yes, that sounds like what she was screaming. I thought she was a street person who was delusional, so I ran."

"My, my! And what was she pointing at before you ran away?"

"Her shopping bag. Then she'd point at me."

"I think you'd better go look in your shopping bag. I think you got hers by mistake." I went back into the kitchen and searched through every bag. Sure enough, there in a generic-looking brown paper bag was a brassiere in a size that could hold two cantaloupes comfortably. I walked back into the dining room holding the black-lace bra.

"Oh, I see!" The count started laughing. "You are only here a day or two and you become kinky. You are already becoming German!"

"If you only knew. The bag that the other woman got stuck with had a pair of handcuffs. I wandered into a store called *der Boss*."

"I see," Siegfreid commented while raising his eyebrows with a look that said "I'm impressed . . . and I'm interested." He motioned to me to grab my bowl of pasta and bring it with me. We went upstairs, and Siegfreid proceeded to dish small amounts of the penne onto different parts of my body and eat it off in a sensuous dining experience I will never forget.

Once I got past the idea of how sticky this could potentially make the sheets, I learned to relax and enjoy the count's food fest. But no matter how hard I tried, I couldn't get over the fact that those handcuffs would have come in handy at that point.

The next morning, the count woke early, ate, showered, and dressed so he could polish off some meetings he said couldn't be avoided. He admonished me to stay in bed and sleep in, since he would be gone most of the day. I followed his advice. I got up later, had a quick breakfast, took a luxurious bath, and was just getting dressed to head out on the town to take in the Pergamon Museum when there was a knock on my door.

"Yes?" I asked.

"It is me, Herr Willsop. Karl. At za door, zair iz man to zee Siegfreid. Heez name he say iz Ludvig."

"Karl, the count is gone on business. I will come down to see him," I said through the safely closed door. (I decided it would be a good idea to keep closed doors between me and Karl as long as the count wasn't around. You never could tell.)

"I vill put heem in za . . . li . . . li . . . how do you zay . . . za room mit da books."

"The library. Thank you, Karl. I'll be right there."

I didn't quite know what to do, but thought as long as I was titular head of the house, I would try and handle the count's affairs as best I could. Dignity above all else, I told myself. Siegfreid's visitor could very well be royalty—some heir of a long-forgotten principality of Prussia or a duke from Austria. As I descended the stairs, walked down the hall and into the library, I found I wasn't far from the truth. Sitting there on one of the leather sofas was a big ol' queen. I was so startled by Siegfreid's guest, I stopped for a moment, then offered my hand as a gesture of friendship.

A hand with rings on every finger poked out of a voluminous caftan and inched its way to offer a limp handshake, but also suggested I should kiss it in the Continental manner of a gentleman to that of a lady. There was no fuckin' way I was going to kiss that hand. I had no idea where it had been, but from the look of it, to several dozen jewelers. So I shook it and sat down on a sofa across from him.

"You are Robert!" he squealed with delight. "Siegfreid, he tell so much to me about you!"

It's at moments like this one that I wished I had a camera to prove to others what I was seeing. You just couldn't make this guy up. Ludwig looked like a very large inmate from a men's prison that had tried to escape a transvestite planet, but never completely broke away from its gravitational pull. Parts of him, like the close-cropped military Mohawk hair-cut, seemed downright butch, but they were outweighed by items such as very false eyelashes and gold brocaded slippers with Arabian Nights curled-up toes. Long, dangling diamond earrings and a caftan bearing a print of Botticelli's *The Birth of Venus* fought with a facial scar for butch supremacy. The earrings and the caftan won.

I had to stop staring and say something. "I'm sorry to tell you Siegfreid isn't here. He's out on business all day. I'm sorry you came all this way for nothing."

"All the time he is gone! I try to see him a lot and I can only talk to him on the phone. He is always out when I come here!" he complained fussily. He reached into a silk purse and retrieved a handkerchief, then blew his nose with a daintiness that would put Queen Elizabeth to shame.

"Perhaps you could tell me why you came and I can convey your message to Siegfreid when he gets home this evening."

"It is business, too. Siegfreid and I have a small . . . what is the word . . . arrangement we have made. I must talk to him about it—man to man."

Man to man, I thought. *In your dreams, honey.* "You mean it's personal?"

"Yes, it is something I can say only to him." He looked as if he were going to say something else, but changed his mind.

"So how long have you known Siegfreid, Ludwig?" I asked. Since the count never really told me a lot about his past, I figured Ludwig could possibly shed some light on this area.

"I have known him twenty years."

"Twenty years, wow! I guess you must know a lot about him, then. What's he like?"

"Oh, he is . . . what is the word . . . popular. Many men

in Berlin want to be his boyfriend, but he says no to them all," Ludwig reported. "You have much luck that you get chosen as his boyfriend. This is not Siegfreid."

"So he's never had a boyfriend?" This didn't sound good, coming from a friend.

"No, he had boyfriends in the past, but most were long ago."

"Long ago?" I inquired.

"Franz was his boyfriend many years, but Franz died ten, eleven years ago. Hans was last one, but count has not dated him for at least a year. Maybe more. Hans moved to Bonn, I think. Or Düsseldorf. I do not remember. You must be lucky for Siegfreid."

"Me? Lucky?" I answered. I can't even associate the word lucky with myself.

"Oh, yes. Before Siegfreid go to United States, he say he is going to look for a boyfriend. Then he finds you! You are lucky, it would seem. Maybe some of your luck would rub off on me if I touch you!" he suggested as his stubby fingers led him to get up and change his seating arrangement. He rose from the sofa and floated around the large coffee table to take his place next to me—uncomfortably close to me. He reached out and traced a finger back and forth across my knee.

"So we must become good friends, yes? Must I wait until I see you at my party next week?"

"Oh my God," I said, finally getting it. "You're Mad Queen . . . er . . . you're having the famous ball! I never connected that you're *that* Ludwig!"

"My name is Ludwig Buxtehude, but you may call me a queen or mad—I am a little of both. But what is bad about being a queen or mad? Call me any name, because I can be any man you wish me to be," he stated, his finger winding its way up toward my crotch. "Yah, Robert? You want me to be Hercules?"

Mad Queen Ludwig, I thought. Boy, his friends didn't

just pick that name out of the air, did they? "I was thinking you were more of a Samson . . . or Salome even!"

"You want me to do my dance of the seven veils?" he said, waving his hand seductively in front of his face as if it were a silk scarf.

Another thought: it would take far more than seven veils to cover this girl. I wondered if they had baseball field tarps in Germany. While I considered this possibility, Ludwig's hand kept up its relentless march across my leg and was quickly joined by his other hand in exploring my body, which decided it would run itself through my hair.

I didn't mean to let Ludwig get this far, but I was trying to be polite. But it was becoming clear I needed to do something fast. I was just about to pull away from Ludwig when the door to the library flew open and there stood Karl, tray in hand and an accusing look on his face. He stood there motionless, in a move calculated to make a fairly innocent scene look guiltier than sin. The overly shocked look on his face was meant to pin the scarlet letter square on my shirt. I wouldn't put it past Karl to have been eavesdropping through the door and peering through the keyhole, waiting for just the right moment to catch me in the act. He was obviously an amateur. A real pro would have had a camera.

"Everything is fine, Karl. You can go now," I said as I waved him away.

"I am zorry, Herr Willsop. I forgot you were in here," he lied through his capped teeth.

"That's OK, Ludwig was just like you . . . in the process of leaving," I replied, hoping Karl would take the hint—and Ludwig, too.

Karl went out, backing through the door, but before he closed it behind him, he turned and flashed me a just-wait-'til-I-tell-daddy look and smiled like he had the goods on me. From now on, Karl couldn't be trusted. And there would be no year-end bonus in his Christmas card.

"Ludwig, I think you need to go. I will let the count know he must call you."

"Yah, you must, Herr Willsop. This is very important. *Very* important," he stressed, putting so much emphasis on the word that it sounded criminal.

I saw Ludwig out, but not without him raising my hand at the door and kissing it like it was the Holy Grail.

"I can't wait to see you at your masquerade ball, Ludwig. Until then," I said, waving him away in his chauffeur-driven, flaming red Rolls Royce—perhaps the only one of its kind in Germany (or existence).

Just as Ludwig was driving away in his chariot of the goddesses, another car drove into the driveway after it and parked. Out jumped a virile-looking German man who started speaking excitedly in German to me. When he saw nothing he said registered on my face, he cocked his head and asked me in almost flawless English, "You are Robert, no?"

"No, I am . . . I mean yes . . . I don't know what I mean."

"My name is Heino. I am Siegfried's business partner. I came to see the count. He is around?"

"No, I'm sorry, Heino. He left a few hours ago on business. I assumed he was with you."

"No, no, he is not with me. I told him I had to see him today and he said he couldn't, that he was on a honeymoon. No business. But I said I had to see him in person."

"If he didn't want to talk with you, why did he tell me that he was going out on business, I wonder?"

"I do not know," Heino answered. "He has been so busy lately. He used to be very much involved in his shipping business, but now he leaves everything to me. I think he wants to settle down and spend time with his new boyfriend," he stated, pointing at me. "I do not blame him. You are so much better than a ship," he said in earnest.

I supposed it was a compliment, but it was a strange one.

I tried to picture a ship that would represent me: The S.S. Neurotic. It wanted to set sail for exotic and exciting places, but never left port because it was afraid something bad might happen.

Heino looked around as if the answer to Siegfreid's whereabouts was scrawled on the face of the count's town house. "Well, I must go now. Please, tell Siegfreid I must talk to him about something urgent. I will try to call him on his cellular phone, but he never answers." Heino reached out and shook my hand good-bye, said he was glad to have met me, and got into his car and departed—leaving me confused.

I went out for a walk, had lunch at a sidewalk café, and returned home around three in the afternoon. I was tired, so I took a nap. My do-nothing lifestyle took more effort than I realized. You didn't just sit around all day eating chocolate bonbons and talking on the telephone to your friends. No, siree. You had to deal with amorous drag queens, hateful servants, snotty chauffeurs, and prying housekeepers.

I had a brief nightmare where Ludwig was wearing a G-string and threatened to take it off. Thankfully I woke up before he could remove the garment—but was confronted with something equally frightening: the sight of Karl standing over me with a pillow in his hands.

"Zorry, Herr Willsop. I vas changing zese sheets in da udder bedrume und braut deese pillow in to gif to you."

I propped myself up on my elbow, still in shock that I had caught Karl trying to smother me while I slept. I was still groggy, so I said the first thing that came into my mind: "Karl, would you bring me a .357 Magnum to put under my pillow?"

Karl looked at me quizzically, then laughed, even though he didn't understand what he was laughing about. "I'm zorry, I do not understand."

"Never mind," I replied.

The minute Karl left, I locked the door to the bedroom and ran to the phone. I dialed the phone and prayed it would be answered.

"Hello? Monette O'Reilley."

"Monette, thank God you were in your office! Karl, one of the servants in the house, just tried to kill me!" I heaved.

"Oh, really," she responded. "Our receptionist tried to stab me and a Mongolian hit man tried to assassinate me this morning. And it's not even noon yet."

"I'm serious, Monette. I just took a nap and when I woke up, Karl was standing over me, holding a pillow he was going to smother me with."

"OK, calm down and tell me the whole story."

I did, embellishing a bit here and there for effect. Who's to say there wasn't a titanic struggle as my arms flailed about, trying to valiantly loosen the pillow from Karl's homicidal clutch of death? Everything is subjective, right? Likewise, Helmut's amorous penne-garnishing episode more correctly reflected his ruthless and cunning nature as a rapacious mantrap.

"My advice to you," Monette started, "is to spend as little time in the house as you can. Or at least whenever Siegfreid is out. Have witnesses."

"What is it about me that makes people want to murder me, Monette? Last year, Michael's mother pushed me down a flight of stairs *and* tried to bean me with a four-hundred-pound painting. Now Karl's trying to snuff me out. Why is it no one ever thinks of snuffing out someone really obnoxious, like Pat Robertson?"

"Or Pat Buchanan?" Monette volunteered. "And Charlton Heston?"

"Yes, thank you, Monette. Why doesn't someone bump him off? I mean, am I that horrible? Look, I've never stolen someone else's cab, I've never taken two trips to the salad bar when there was a one-trip limit, and I've never given anyone the crabs. I ought to get a lifetime achievement award for being so nice to others."

"Like I said," Monette continued, "stay out of the house whenever Siegfreid isn't around. And go have fun."

"But Siegfreid's always gone. Plus, listen to this. Heino, his business manager came to see him today for an appointment and Siegfreid was out. The count made no mention of being here to see Heino."

"So what's your point?" Monette inquired.

"The point is, the count is supposed to be with Heino on business and he's not. Heino was looking for *him*."

Monette's voice began to take on a motherly tone. "Did you ever think he could be out on business somewhere else? He doesn't have to be with Heino."

"Yes, but I never know where he is. And neither does anyone else. Everyone's remarking that he's been very secretive lately. He's never here at the house and none of his friends have seen much of him lately. I'm beginning to think he's having an affair with some other guy during the day."

Monette jumped to cross-examine my theory. "But why go all the way to America to get you as a boyfriend, then drag you back to Germany and have affairs on you? It doesn't make any sense. He could probably have any guy he wants right there. Why bring you in to complicate matters?"

"Good point, Monette. I just wish I knew where he was during the day." I sighed.

"I know this is going to seem very radical, but why don't you just ask him?"

"You're right! I will. As soon as he comes home, I'm going to confront him. In fact, I think his car is pulling into the driveway right now."

"Well, go to him. Call me back tomorrow and let me know what you've found out."

"I don't know if I can. We're leaving for Monte Carlo tomorrow," I said.

"Then leave a message on my machine. OK?"

"It's a deal, Monette. And if I don't talk to you before I leave, I'll see you here in Berlin the day of Ludwig's ball. Did you get the tickets and itinerary? I sent them FedEx."

"I got everything."

"I gotta go now, Monette. I'll leave you a message."

"*Auf wiedersehen*, Robert."

I hung up the phone and ran downstairs to meet Siegfreid as he came in the door. I threw my arms around him and planted a very wet kiss on his lips.

"Well, well, I must go out on business more often if I come home and get a reception like this!" he exclaimed.

"I just missed you, Siegfreid. Don't leave me again . . ." *so that Karl doesn't kill me*, I was going to say, but left it as I did. OK, it was time for the confrontation. Easy now. No guilt. Go!

"Siegfreid?"

"Yes, Robert?"

"I never know where you are when you go."

"Does that bother you?" he asked with genuine concern.

"A little. But it's . . . inconvenient. Mad Queen Ludwig and Heino stopped by today, and I couldn't tell them where you were. Heino thought he was supposed to meet you here. They both had something urgent to discuss with you."

Siegfreid looked like he was debating whether to tell me something earthshaking, fell silent, then picked up his briefcase and pulled out a small, beautifully wrapped package and handed it to me.

"I was going to save this to give you in Monte Carlo, but I think you need it now, yes? Go ahead, open it!"

I was flabbergasted and a little bit ashamed. This must have been what Siegfreid was up to. I opened the gift and inside was a jewelry box, small enough to contain a ring. I opened the box and sure enough, there was a ring. Simple, tasteful, and unimaginably expensive, I would assume, judging from the exquisite box and packaging.

"Oh, Siegfreid, I don't know what to say!" I gushed.

"Just put it on . . . and it will match the one I have on," he commanded, showing me the identical ring on his finger.

OK, so I wouldn't ask him where he had been. Maybe never. The ring quieted me down for now. He had obviously gone to a lot of trouble to get two rings custom made for us. I'm sure that took time.

We had dinner that night, with Helmut getting in a few quick sleight of hands, such as letting his hand slide over Siegfreid's while spooning an entrée onto his dish, or my favorite: After pouring wine for the count, Helmut would walk around behind Siegfreid and drag a finger seductively across the count's upper back. But I, like the count, had learned to treat Helmut's advances the way the count did. I ignored them.

After dinner, we packed for Monte Carlo. Then Siegfreid excused himself for a few moments to make a phone call.

As I was packing tuxedos from the count's closet, I discovered Siegfreid had at least a dozen different styles. I walked down the hall to Siegfreid's makeshift office and knocked lightly on the door.

"No, no . . . in English, Ludwig. You need to learn better English. No, no more money," came Siegfreid's angry voice from the other side of the door. "No, no, you've spent enough already. No, I can't give you my entire fortune because you've made some bad mistakes. No. That is the end. I must go. Make do with what I gave you. I am going to Monte Carlo tomorrow. No more. *Auf wiedersehen.*"

I tapped a little louder on the door. "Yes?" Siegfreid called exasperatedly.

"Siegfreid, it's me . . . Robert," I answered as I timidly pushed the door open. The count's face had lost its youthful color and now looked red and irritated.

"Robert, Robert. What is it?" he said without acknowledging his little conversation a minute ago.

"I was wondering which tuxedo you wanted to bring. You have so many!"

"We must go back to find one that looks closest to the one you just bought. Let us go."

His talk with Ludwig was dropped and never mentioned.

He helped me finish packing, then initiated a little hanky-panky before bed. The count went right to sleep, but I stayed awake for a while, thinking. What would Monte Carlo be like? Would I look like Sean Connery sitting around a baccarat table placing one hundred thousand dollar bets? Were there really surveillance cameras on every street corner?

More importantly, why was Ludwig asking the count for more money when he was supposed to be a wealthy man himself? As I pondered these questions in my head, another thought occurred to me that I felt I had to act on immediately. I got up out of bed and locked the door to the bedroom . . . just in case Karl decided to slip in during the night and strangle me with the cord to my electric razor. And just to make sure, I pushed a chair back up under the doorknob and wedged it there. I'd think of something to explain to Siegfreid about the chair in the morning.

8

What's Good Enough for Princess Grace Is Good Enough for You

The next morning, we had breakfast, showered and shaved, and gathered up our things for the flight to Monte Carlo. As we were standing at the door of the palace and heading toward the car, Siegfreid summoned Karl and Helmut and announced he would give them a few days off while we were gone. He peeled off a generous amount of cash from the wad of bills in his pocket and told them to have a good time.

The flight itself to Monte Carlo was uneventful, except for the sex we had in the bathroom of the count's chartered jet. Twice. Sex was becoming such a regular part of my life that I was now taking it for granted. In all my life, I never thought such a situation would occur.

We stayed in a villa in the hills overlooking the casinos because the count said it would be more private there. I couldn't argue, since it was stunning and the views were breathtaking. We had sex throughout the day and went into the casinos one night to gamble. The count taught me to play baccarat, and I did, with opening bids starting at one thousand dollars. I actually finished the evening fourteen thousand dollars ahead. For the first time in my life, I was a winner—and I had proof.

The next day, the count and I decided to take a drive up

in the winding mountainous roads above Monte Carlo. The count was flying down the roads a little too fast for me when the car sputtered, coughed, and died, coming to rest on a stretch of road with few houses.

I thought of sticking my leg out like Claudette Colbert in *It Happened One Night* to stop a car, but decided it wasn't worth the effort. With my luck, someone would run over it.

We stood at the edge of the road waiting for someone to stop when I spotted a cloud of dust racing toward us. It approached us, then flew past in a whirlwind of dirt, sticks, and rocks. Just then, I heard a squeal of brakes as the vintage sports car skidded gracefully to a stop a few hundred feet down the road. I saw the passenger excitedly tapping the driver on the shoulder and motioning for her to back up. The driver did and produced another cloud of dust, screaming back toward us until the car stopped abruptly just feet away. In the car were none other than Michael Stark and his covertly vicious mother, Julia.

Normally I would have been elated to not only meet a friend in a foreign land and get roadside assistance to boot, but Julia and I had a brief but homicidal run-in the one and only time I stayed at Michael's ancestral family estate in Newport, Rhode Island.

Julia, who had a past as checkered as an Italian restaurant tablecloth, was the unfortunate victim of circumstances that repeatedly put her in the close vicinity of several accidental deaths on her estate. Unfortunate, I say—it's unfortunate Julia wasn't better at covering her tracks. But, as they say, money talks, and when you practically poop it, little things like messy and dubious deaths get brushed under priceless Persian rugs. So despite the fact Michael had been sexually entangled with each of the victims and Julia wanted no part of her son to be gay, I will lay the facts at the feet of you, the jury, and let you make up your own mind. I won't even mention the fact that during my one-night stay at End

House (the Stark residence) in Newport, Rhode Island, I was pushed down a flight of stairs and almost clobbered by a huge painting (of Julia, ironically) that would have made my brain come out of my ears like watery guacamole. So it was not without some trepidation that I stood here face to face with Julia, once again within striking distance.

"Robin, so glad to see you again." Julia beamed at me as if she had been pounding down sidecars since breakfast. When I looked at the unfinished highball glass wedged in between the seats, I knew I might not be far from the truth. The woman hated me, but liquor seemed to make her unusually sociable.

"Robert," I corrected her. "So nice to see you again, Mrs. Stark."

"Julia, please. You can call me by my first name, Robin. Do either of you know where to find an Episcopalian church in this blasted country? There don't seem to be anything but Catholic churches here."

The count and I shrugged our shoulders.

While Julia prided herself on possessing wealth that could crush a third-world country, her social position, and unbreakable alibis, one of her greatest achievements was that she was also an Episcopalian—one of God's frozen people.

"So lucky us meeting you here!" Michael remarked.

"The coincidence is amazing. Truly amazing!" the count added.

"Oops, I'm sorry, Siegfreid, I haven't introduced you. You know Michael, and this," I said, motioning to Mrs. Stark, "is Mrs. Stabb. This, Julia, is Count Siegfreid von Schmidt."

"Robert!" Michael chastised me. "You just called my mother Mrs. Stabb. What would make you think that?"

I have no idea, Michael, I thought to myself, *but I'm sure Dr. Freud would have plenty to say.*

Julia extended her limp and jewel-encrusted hand for the count to shake, but the count gently lifted the murderous appendage and kissed it in the Continental style.

"It is a pleasure meeting you, Julia," the count said so seductively that her gay-hating nature seemed somewhat subdued. *Somewhat*, I said.

"Well, it looks like you two could use a lift," Julia said. "There's not a lot of room, but jump in. This is the exact same car Grace Kelley drove in *To Catch A Thief*. Oh, poor Grace! Right over that cliff! What a loss! She was the closest thing to royalty the United States will ever have."

I wasn't about to let this one slip by. "Whatever happened to Camelot? I thought Jackie Kennedy was quite regal," I replied, defending the holy name of Jackie O. After all, I am a faggot who realizes her enormous contribution to the world: the pillbox hat and elbow-length gloves.

"My dear Robin . . ."

"Robert, Mrs. Stark. *Robert*," I said, correcting the winner of the 2001 Passive Aggressive Bitch Award again.

"Robert, as you probably know, Jackie lived for some time in Newport, and if I told you what I really knew about her and those awful Kennedys, you'd never vote Democrat again. Her behavior was neither queenlike *nor* royal."

I was going to reply with something nonconfrontational, such as, "Fat chance, you rapacious, hateful harpy," but decided it wasn't a good idea to upset her, as she was about to have our lives in her desiccated and pampered hands. So I said nothing, letting her think she had won yet another battle.

As Julia looked misty-eyed at the principality of Monte Carlo thousands of feet below us, we climbed into the tiny jump seat in the back of the car and the auto roared to life, Julia's spectator shoes pressing down on the gas pedal as if a welfare mother's head was beneath it.

Michael babbled on and on about nothing in particular

while the count politely half listened and half raised his head up into the breeze that whistled through his hair. Me, I sat white-knuckled and gripped with terror, sensing Julia could plunge the car off the side of a cliff and accomplish two things at once: one, to die in the same manner as the exalted Ice Queen, Princess Grace, and, two, to take three faggots with her at the same time—an all-time record. After all, why bother snuffing them out one by one and arousing suspicion in Newport when you can make it all look like a tragic accident and get some newspaper coverage at the same time?

Miraculously, we made it back to Monte Carlo and our hotel without a scratch. The count, gracious as always, invited Julia and Michael into our hotel lobby for some drinks and they accepted.

We were sitting around chatting when Michael asked me to go to the bathroom with him.

"Michael," I said, turning aside to him and speaking in a lower tone of voice so Julia wouldn't hear me, "you need help adjusting your tampon? I'll get some pliers and meet you in the third stall."

"No, I just need to ask you something. Let's move!" Michael said, excusing us and leaving the count and Julia alone.

Michael was so excited that the moment we were out of sight of the lobby, he blurted out what was on his mind—a frightening thought.

"You have to get me an invitation to Mad Queen Ludwig's party! A little birdie told me you two received one. It's *the* hottest party in the universe! Oh God, please get me an invite, *danke*?"

"Michael, *danke* means thank you. *Bitte* means please. I'll mention it to the count. I'm sure it will be no problem."

"And I have something else to ask you."

"What is it, Michael?"

"Please take me with you . . . like right now. My mother is driving me nuts! We went gambling last night and she won fifty-seven thousand dollars. I lost forty-two thousand dollars, so that was kind of fun. But the rest of it I can't stand. She watches me all the time and she's always dragging me to some art museum or something *cultural*!"

"Well . . ." I said, not wanting to let Michael crowd in on my honeymoon. I figured as soon as I left the door open to Michael, a condom wouldn't be the only thing between myself and the count. As much as the thought of a familiar face in a strange country would be nice, it would be better if it weren't Michael's.

"Michael, this is a personal matter, so I need to talk to the count about it first," I said, lying through my teeth. I had no intention of asking the count in private. I would just tell Michael the count said *nein*.

"Fine," Michael replied. "Let's go back."

"But don't you have to pee, Michael?"

"There aren't any cute guys in the loo right now, so why bother?"

"Well, I for one have to be a freak and use this room for the purpose for which it was designed. I'll meet you back in the lobby," I said.

I finished my business and rejoined the others. Michael was in the middle of a conversation. Once I gathered what he was saying, I realized I had just been duped.

". . . so I'd love to continue to travel with you, Mom, but Robert has *insisted* I join him and the count on the rest of their tour and accompany them back to Germany so I can attend the arts festival there."

Before I could say a word about Michael's dubious dubbing of Mad Queen Ludwig's party as an arts festival, the count stepped in and sealed the deal with the devil.

"Whatever Robert wants, Robert gets!" the count announced, with Julia looking at me with those another-piece-of-trailer-trash-makes-good eyes. "You can join us to-morrow, Michael. We're returning to Germany tomorrow and you can fly with us on our plane. There, Robert! Happy?" the count asked.

"Deliriously," was my answer.

9

I Haven't Got a Thing to Wear

The flight back to Germany was uneventful. Uneventful because Michael's presence put a certain damper on things. Much to my chagrin, the bathroom was used only as a bathroom. I began to wonder if it was a bad idea to open the door to the plane at twenty-nine thousand feet and ask Michael to take a walk.

When we got to the count's palace in Berlin, Michael stared up at the hulking façade and acted like he was staring at a one-bedroom co-op on Twenty-third Street. There was not one shred of envy on his chemical-peeled face. And why should there be? His childhood house in Newport, Rhode Island, was monstrous.

The count had some business he had to attend to, so he left me in the house with Michael. When Michael was fully ensconced in his bedroom, I paid him a visit.

"Come in, Herr Schmidt," Michael said through the door.

I entered and found Michael unpacking.

"What the hell is that?" I said after seeing an outfit covered with an ocean of tiny gold beads. "Liberace's nightshirt?"

"Robert, this is my costume for the ball! I'm going as a matador. This outfit really shows off my ass."

"I see. Michael?"

"Yes, Robert?"

"Do you always travel around with a matador's costume?"

"No. Just when I'm going to a masked ball."

"Michael, when you came to Europe, you weren't invited to Mad Queen Ludwig's. But you brought a costume anyway?"

"That's right. Be prepared," Michael said, lovingly hanging up the outfit and putting it in a closet.

"Michael! You came to Europe knowing you would cajole me into snagging an invitation to Ludwig's ball for you!"

"Well, the thought had crossed my mind," Michael said coyly.

"Your plan seemed pretty far-fetched. I guess it was lucky you were driving by our broken down car in Monte Carlo at just that moment. Otherwise your whole plan would have fallen through." Ha! I had figured out Michael's plan at last.

"Who said it was luck that we drove by?" Michael asked without taking his eyes off a leather codpiece he lifted from his suitcase and put in a nearby drawer.

I was speechless, but I managed to get two words out. "You mean?"

"Robert, don't be so Midwestern! I planned the whole thing. I found out where you two were vacationing in Europe, I followed you to Monte Carlo, paid a guy to put sugar in the gas tank of your car, then got Mother to take the sports car out and pass by you two when you were stranded. It may have taken me six years to get through college, but I'm not dumb!"

"You did all this just to get an invitation to a masquerade ball?"

"Mad Queen Ludwig's party is the hippest party in the galaxy. I've known guys who have thrown themselves off rooftops because they didn't get an invitation. Of course, they were flying high on crystal at the time."

"That's pathetic, Michael. I've never even heard of this party."

"That's what makes it so fantastic, Robert! Very few people know about it . . . just the chicest people in the world. They fly in from around the globe under great secrecy. The guest list is handpicked by Ludwig and voted on by a handful of his secret friends. It's all very hush-hush."

"If it's such a secret, then how do you know about it?" I asked.

"I slept with this guy and he offered to get me in."

"It didn't work, did it?"

"Would I be standing here talking to you if it had?"

"Probably not," I admitted.

"So, Robert, what are you wearing to the costume party tonight?"

"You'll see tonight. It's a surprise."

I looked out of the window of Michael's room and noticed a Mercedes sedan with dark windows pull through the open gates and nose its way into the front courtyard. A towering redhead bumped her head on the low doorway as she emerged, shouted a few expletives, struggled with several ragtag suitcases, then stood looking up at the façade of the house.

"Monette's here!" I practically screamed. I opened the window and shouted down to one of the most welcome faces I have ever seen. "Just a minute, Monette, I'll be right down," I yelled.

"You gave up your roach-infested studio apartment in New York for this? Sometimes I just don't understand you, Robert. Oh, and bring a cocktail. The flight was bumpy."

I ran down the stairs, leaving Michael behind. When I reached Monette, she threw her arms around me and lifted me clear in the air. It was the first time a lesbian had swept me off my feet.

"My, my, my, you look great!" Monette said.

"It's only been a week, Monette."

"Yeah, but you wear marriage well. So how was your grand tour of Europe? See a lot?"

"Actually, a lot of ceilings."

"The Sistine Chapel?"

"No, but I did see God several times."

"*Those* ceilings! I see," Monette said, finally getting what I was talking about. "You little rascal, you," she said, waving a naughty finger at me. "How's everything else? The count still treating you well?"

"I don't know. The only thing we've done is make love."

"Don't complain about the sex, Robert. Droughts always follow floods. I know. My vagina is going to be known as the second great Dust Bowl."

"Thank you, Monette, for giving me too much information—especially to a gay man. And speaking about another man who is foreign to a vagina, Michael's here."

"Michael? Here?"

"That's what I said. He stalked me to Monte Carlo, set me up, tricked us into freeing him from his rapacious mother, and now he's upstairs unpacking a latex tank top, if my memory serves me correctly."

"He's not wearing *that* to the ball tonight, is he?" Monette asked, fearful of the idea of walking into any place on earth with Michael "in costume." You never knew what he might wear.

"No, no, he's going as a matador because he can display his ass and show some good box at the same time. It's two, two-man lures in one. Speaking of costumes, did you bring yours?" I inquired.

"It's right here in this suitcase," she said, patting a piece of baggage that looked like it had gone twenty-three rounds with Steve Austin at a World Wrestling Federation smackdown—and lost. Black friction tape was apparently the only thing holding it together.

"So what's the costume?" I asked, dying to know what Lynette had whipped up.

"I don't know. She wins award after award for costume design, so it's gotta be something spectacular. She didn't want me to open it until the last moment, but I guess I could sort of peek at it now," she rationalized, but I cut her off.

"Monette, I've got so much to show you, why don't we do this costume thing later? I'm sure you're famished, so why don't we do lunch first? Then we can do a tour of the house and Siegfried will be home by then. He's off on some business this morning."

"Sounds good to me. As long as you don't try and make me eat sauerkraut," Monette added, noting one of two things in life that terrified her. The other was clowns—she had a mortal fear of them.

"No problem. The count's latest cook is strictly into nouvelle Italian cuisine. I think I've died and gone to heaven!"

I showed Monette to her room and told her to take a few minutes to freshen up. To which she responded, "Freshen up? From what?"

"I don't know. Go do something ladylike," I instructed her.

We all met in the cavernous dining room, ate a delicious lunch, and finished off two bottles of a wonderful German wine.

After lunch, I took Monette and Michael on a tour. Since the only rooms I knew well were the bedroom, bathroom, and the kitchen, most of what I saw was a complete surprise to me.

And surprises there were. There was a small movie theater in the basement, an indoor pool, a cocktail bar with a trompe l'oeil mural designed to make you feel you were at a Parisian café, a mini bowling alley, and a shooting range complete with guns housed in locked cases.

We nosed around, not quite sure whether we were snooping beyond the bounds of propriety, but we felt that if we came upon anything too risqué or private, we could back out and pretend we hadn't seen anything. Monette and I got in the spirit of things.

"What's behind this door?" Monette asked, trying the knob to a particularly scary-looking door with heavy locks. "I suppose this is where you keep the servants locked up." The door was locked.

"Probably a dungeon," Michael finally spoke up.

Since Michael couldn't remember whom he had slept with the previous day, history was not one of his strong suits. "Michael, this house was destroyed in the war. It isn't from the 1600s."

"No, no, prude Robert. A sex room! A playroom! You know, there are people who get bored with vanilla sex. There's nothing wrong with adding a little spanking to spice things up!"

"I wouldn't talk, Michael. You can brag all you want about your outlandish sex acts, but I know for a fact you have good old-fashioned vanilla sex from time to time."

"Yes, Robert, but even my vanilla is chocolate!" Michael responded, licking his lips naughtily. "Don't act so innocent. You told me yourself you like to pinch your nipples and fantasize about gladiators sometimes," Michael said, perhaps giving Monette a little too much information. The evil smile on her face said it definitely was the wrong kind of information to put into her hands.

Monette opened another door and peered in. "Whoops!" she said. "Must be one of the servant's rooms."

"No, it can't be, Monette. Almost all of the servants work during the day and go home at night. Even the cook leaves by nine."

"Well it looks like someone left their belongings here. They must've left in a hurry, because there are some clothes and a lot of videotapes."

"The count fired the whole staff before he came to America. He says you can't find good help, especially in Berlin. The servant must have had just enough time to grab a few things, a paycheck, and run."

"I know how Siegfreid feels," Michael added. "I can't keep a manservant. I fired my last one because I caught him smelling my shorts," Michael said, as if this happened every day.

"My God," I exclaimed. "That's repulsive!"

"I know. I thought this guy was weird, but the one before him took the cake. He was having sex with red ants in my apartment."

Monette couldn't let this one go by. "Red ants? Aren't they kind of small . . . and don't they explode when you have an orgasm?"

"He'd put a jar of red ants on his crotch and they'd bite him and he'd get off on it."

Monette and I stood there completely dumbfounded. I was going to ask where the manservant got red ants in New York City, but I figured that would lead into a discussion of a kinky underground supply system I didn't want to know existed. Instead, I merely replied, "Michael, someday I'm going to have to hurt you really badly for telling me this. Now, where were we?"

Monette spoke up. "I think we were poking our noses around the count's house. Maybe we should poke around town instead," she said, not without a little begging in her voice.

"I have a better idea. Why don't we take a spin in my new car?" I said, as Monette gave me a thumbs-up gesture.

We drove around the city having the time of our lives. Or at least, Monette and I were enjoying ourselves, drinking in the history that seemed to be around every corner. Michael played the part of the Ugly American, claiming he didn't see why they called it the Brandenburg Gate when there wasn't any gate visible and was mystified that Berlin was ever divided into East and West. He did, however, pay plenty of attention to the men of Berlin. He ogled scores of men from the moving car, his head turning around more times than Linda Blair's in *The Exorcist*.

I had no way of knowing it then, but a priest would've come in handy later on that evening.

10

I'd Kill to Get into this Party

When we got back to the palace, we found the count smoking a large cigar in the trophy room, which was replete with animal heads no doubt collected from hunts around the world. We decided since there wasn't enough time before the ball, we would just sit around and listen to jazz, talk, and have cocktails.

We had a light meal, then went to our rooms to begin dressing for a night that would live in infamy.

A half hour later, there was a knock at the door. I opened it and was confronted with the most horrific thing I have ever seen since catching a glimpse of Liza Minelli after a week-long lasagna binge.

Monette was standing at my door, drumming her fingers and sporting a just-wait-till-I-get-you-back-for-this look. She was dressed in a skintight outfit made from purple leather with yellow leather piping around the pockets. The waistcoat, which was cinched at the waist and flared out at the bottom, was complemented by matching tight pants that flared out into two-foot bellbottoms. The pièce de résistance was modeled from one of those mushroom-puff hats that decorated such blaxploitation films such as *Cleopatra Jones*. Of course, Lynette had done her job fully and made a purple leather mask (with yellow flames shooting out from the eyes) in keeping with Ludwig's request that each guest remain anonymous.

For two whole minutes, I snorted and stifled laughs, trying not to let Monette on to the fact I had set her up with Lynette's help back in New York, but the jig was definitely up.

"Why, Monette!" I shrieked. "This must be the latest from the new designer—Osh-Kosh-B'Gosh!"

"I deserved this for getting you at your bon voyage party in New York," she said, her face smiling and admitting defeat. Temporarily. "I promise you, I will get you back for this. Do you think I'll stand out in this?"

"I think with your height and those five-inch multicolored matching wedgies, you couldn't fail. I'd watch out for low doorways, though."

"You know I'm going in this outfit, Robert," Monette said defiantly. "I can dish it out, but I want you to know that I can bend over and take it like a gay man."

"It's good to see you being so mature about being defeated so resoundingly, Monette. Now, could you excuse me? Siegfried and I have to get dressed in our fabulous outfits. We'll meet you downstairs."

I closed the door and cackled like Bette Davis probably did the day she opened up *The New York Times* and saw Joan Crawford's obituary. The only difference between me and the late Miss Davis was that I didn't have time to open a bottle of champagne.

A little background on Mad Queen Ludwig. It's no joke. He really is a direct descendant of Mad King Ludwig, who erected Neuschwanstein, the famous and astutely located castle in Bavaria that still bears his name. I still don't know why anyone could doubt the rumors about Louis II being gay. Only a gay man would find a spot *that* perfect to build on.

Ludwig Buxtehude was raised in the lap of luxury, but instead of remaining reserved and keeping a low profile like most royalty, he began dressing in women's clothes at a very early age. His parents turned a blind eye to Ludwig's shenanigans at first, chalking up his behavior to the genetic madness that ensured that more than one cuckoo nested in the family tree. Over time, as his outfits became more and more elaborate, his parents felt that his outlandish behavior could no longer be ignored any more than you could an elephant in a living room.

His parents tried to get him into the best all-girls school in Germany, which caused some speculation that the insanity in the family wasn't just confined to Ludwig himself. Anyway, the effort failed and his parents did something even more foolish: they enrolled him in an all-boys academy in Stuttgart. Ludwig went boy-crazy and was expelled, leaving his mother and father with only one choice, to tutor him at home and keep his outrageous behavior out of the limelight. Their decision backfired and, like mold prospering in an airless environment, Ludwig grew out of control and became known far and wide as the biggest flamer in Germany.

After his parents died and he had shoveled dirt onto the coffin of his last relative, Ludwig put the pedal to the metal and began living a stratospheric lifestyle that tore through a family fortune that took centuries of swindling to amass. But Ludwig didn't care. Who would he leave it to, anyway? He also began throwing outrageous parties that allowed him to act out his whims and get praise for them at the same time, forming the basis for his famous masquerade ball. The rest is history.

An hour after I had vanquished Monette, Siegfreid and I descended the stairs, he dressed as Marc Anthony and I as a gladiator. What could I say? Siegfreid asked me what I wanted to go as, and I told him. My costume, which cost a fortune, was cleverly padded and gave me the appearance of being extremely muscular. The count burst into laughter when he saw Monette for the first time, apologized for laughing, then started up again. He was soon wiping tears from his eyes.

Michael, a man dressed in a skintight matador costume, looked at mine and said, "Robert, the gladiator look is so last year!"

"And what makes matadors so *in*?" I challenged Michael.

"Great asses are always in, Robert!" Michael said as if he were quoting the pages of *GQ*. I could see the headline now: *Asses In! Ancient Romans Out!*

We gathered ourselves up, went out into the courtyard, and stepped into a vintage convertible Cadillac limousine in shocking red which whisked us to Ludwig's palace (and it was a palace) outside of Berlin. The driveway was full of the oddest assortment of numerous limousines, carriages, a humvee, and a tiny Mercedes ahead of us that was covered with thousands of tiny square mirrors, making it look like a drivable disco ball.

As we left the limousine and climbed the stairs, the assortment of people was equally bizarre. Siegfreid said Ludwig's party originally started out as a mere masked costume ball, with fabulous renditions of seventeenth-century dukes and duchesses as the norm. But as the quiet fame of the ball spread, guests began to outdo each other and the extravagances snowballed out of control. Before you knew it, guests were riding in on zebras and having motorized this and electrical that. Mad Queen Ludwig felt it was time to lay down some rules, not just because of the tremendous legal liability he was incurring, but—the real reason, Siegfreid explained—that there was only one queen at this party and that queen was Ludwig.

As we passed by the impeccably dressed but deadly looking security guards at the top of the stairs and entered the palace ballroom, people began to look at Monette's outfit and whisper among themselves until some were outright pointing at Monette. Being no stranger to raising eye-brows, my defeated lesbian sidekick kept her head held high. People didn't know what to make of her attire. The ice was broken by an extremely stylish man who walked up to her and said with an accent of unfathomable origin, "My dear, wherever did you get zis outfit? It is zee most twisted and decadent apparel I have ever zeen!" he screamed, dar-ing to run his hand over the purple monstrosity. "It's fabu-lous!"

Monette didn't know what to say. "Thank you, I suppose."

Our stylish gentleman reached up and raised Monette's hand high in a triumphant gesture to show off the outfit to its fullest. "Ladies and gentlemen, izn't it spectacularrrrr?" he exclaimed, rolling the last few r's that made him sound like Eartha Kitt riding in a car with no shocks.

You wouldn't believe it, but a good fifty people standing nearby burst into applause. I even heard a bravo from the crowd. I pull an incredible practical joke on Monette, and she ends up as belle of the ball.

The count introduced himself to no one, but plenty of people came up to him, despite his mask. These people were all smiles and kisses, but the moment they discovered they were talking to Count Siegfreid von Schmidt, their personalities changed—and not for the better.

A man with huge muscles dressed as some sort of strong-man started begging the count to give him more money. "If you don't, they will take away my furniture, Siegfreid!' he pleaded. The count waved him aside.

Two men started a fistfight over the count—well, techni-cally it was a catfight/slapfest. As the two of them were led away by the security guards who appeared from nowhere, they continued to slap and accuse each other in French and English of pushing the other aside in an attempt to sink their claws into the count.

One guy, after finding out I was the count's new lover, even muttered what had to be some German expletives before walking away. I knew very little German, but I certainly knew what *scheisskopf* (shithead) meant. It was the first German word I learned, since it was so handy.

"He's just jealous," the count said. "Many of these people have been my boyfriend—or want to be. And you, dear Robert, have come along and taken their place! They want a life of leisure and material things, and you have come in and brushed them aside and ruined their plans!" The count laughed.

I was the only one who wasn't laughing.

People were soon flocking around Monette, trying to ascertain who she was and where she came from. The count, from time to time, acted as interpreter for Monette, who spoke little of any dialect except English and a little south Boston. I couldn't understand everything Siegfreid said, but Monette was clearly having a field day, telling the crowd unbelievable whoppers. She claimed she was raised in Fiji by natives after her mother, a newspaper heiress named Rainbow, had flown there in a single-engine Cessna stunt plane to avoid a jealous husband, an outlaw cowboy named Pecos Sam. Her completely over-the-top fabricated history wouldn't have stood a chance in the U.S., but it went over like gangbusters with a crowd that had long ago lost touch with reality.

When she was done spinning her story, she stopped to give the count a kiss on the cheek, but an inebriated guest bumped into Siegfreid and knocked the mask from his face. The count hurriedly picked up his mask and replaced it, saying, "This is a masquerade party, and we mustn't have people know our real identity! It would take away all the fun!"

Monette pulled me aside for a second and muttered into my ear.

"My god, Siegfreid is handsome! I got a good look at his face for the first time and he is just stunning. The green eyes, the square jaw, the perfect complexion, and topped off by that gorgeous blond hair!"

"Natural blond, too!" I added, about to unleash a dirty secret. "Unlike Michael, who dyes his black."

"You mean unlike the natural gray-red-blonde that just walked by? Sorry, I couldn't let that one go by. Did you see that? His hairdresser obviously is a vicious queen extracting revenge for lousy tips."

Just then, the lights went down and the crowd oohed and aahed, knowing the festivities were about to begin. The ballroom fell silent as a curtain at one end of the football-field-sized ballroom parted and twenty or thirty practically nude men strode out with long, brass trumpets in hand. On cue, they raised their trumpets and issued a blast of notes that would raise the dead. You could feel the excitement in the crowd that expected that something big was going to happen. The trumpeters stepped aside and, to the tune of the latest thumping German trance music, Mad Queen Ludwig rode into view in a gilded carriage pulled by a team of eighteen nude men dressed as horses, complete with feathered bridles, wedge shoes designed to look like horse hooves, and horse tails stuck in their bare asses (held in by God knows what). It had the decadence of the court of Louis the XIV and the flamboyance of a Liberace Vegas act. Siegfreid and Roy would have been jealous. You couldn't see Ludwig himself, because he was obscured by a curtain in the carriage. The only part of him visible was a lilting hand waving a lace handkerchief back and forth.

The carriage was pulled up a specially prepared stairway at one end of the ballroom and circled the wrap-around balcony several times to the wild cheers and clapping of the revelers below. Eventually, the carriage stopped at the top of the stairs at the other end of the ballroom and a man clad in scanty livery rushed to open the door and bow to the famous passenger.

The crowd was now shouting so loudly I thought my eardrums were going to collapse. Finally, Mad Queen Ludwig emerged from the carriage in a magnificent rendition of a royal gown from Elizabethan times. The dress was covered with what must have been hundreds of pearls and brocade work that no doubt made several seamstresses go blind from the intricate stitching. And there, on top of it all, was the head of Mad Queen Ludwig, rising up from a cloud of ironed lace and powdered white like the Virgin Queen herself. He stood there for what seemed an eternity, waving royally to the crowd that roared like a gay freight train.

Just as the crowd's insane cheering seemed about to shatter every mirror in the palace, Ludwig slowly rose into the air and began swinging in a large circle over his guests below, still waving like, well, a queen. Even though the wire that supported him was clearly visible, no one in the crowd seemed to mind. People around me looked up into the heavens as if they were witnessing the Second Coming, albeit with pearls. And I had to admit to myself it was the most outrageous and decadent event I had ever seen—and probably ever will. So much better than a bunch of sissies tweaked on coke or crystal, throwing attitude and bumping into you at a Manhattan nightclub.

Ludwig eventually floated down into his adoring crowds, signifying his fifteen minutes of fame had ended and it was time for the floodgate of cocktails to open and the dancing to begin.

While Monette continued to be the chicest thing this side of Mercury, I was about as welcome as a yeast infection at a NOW convention. Michael, despite a string of bad dates, was bumping into scores of men he had slept with and was looking for some repeat performances. Here I was at the most fashionable party in the world, yet I just wanted to go home. The count, seeing the look of desperation on my face, looked and me and said, "I know what would make you happy!" as he looked down at his crotch.

"Another cocktail would be helpful," I suggested. The count, by the way, seemed to have had quite a few already, and I have to say this was the first time I had ever seen him tipsy.

He grabbed me by my reluctant hand and dragged me to the second floor, where he found a linen closet and pulled me inside. He began to kiss me ravenously, then covered his mouth and exclaimed, "Excuse me, Robert, but I am not feeling well. I have to run downstairs to the bathroom!" He flung the door to the closet open and left me there with my pants undone.

When Siegfreid failed to return after twenty minutes, I went to search for him. I descended the stairs and made for the bathroom, thinking if he had to barf, hopefully he would have made it to the toilet. I approached the men's room conveniently placed off the main ballroom and was about to enter when Mad Queen Ludwig barreled past me like Anna Nicole Smith in search of another boob job. His face was beet red and he was waving his arms around wildly, screaming and holding his throat. Since Ludwig's only method of communication seemed to be screaming or shrieking, no one paid any attention at first. But when he continued screaming, then began to collapse like a glacier plunging in slow motion into the Gulf of Alaska, I knew something wasn't right. I hesitated about going in by myself, but since there were so many people at the ball, I felt it was safe enough to enter.

I left Ludwig as someone was holding his head, trying to get a martini down his gullet, and crept slowly into the lavatory. When I rounded a corner, I saw the body of the count lying with his head in a toilet and a rather large knife in his back. The next thing I remember was the room spinning around and myself falling to the floor, but not before I thought enough to cushion my head and face from the hard marble. My boyfriend was obviously dead, but one had to be practical in matters like this. After all, you had to protect the porcelain.

11

Someone Killed His Boyfriend. Now When's Breakfast?

When I came to, I was surrounded by a dozen people. Closest to me was Monette, who was holding my hand, patting it as if that was going to wake me up. Actually, I was hoping for another sour-apple martini. In every movie I've ever seen, they always revived people with alcohol and it always seemed to do the trick.

"Robert? Robert? C'mon now," Monette pleaded. "Come out of it, sweetie. Don't leave me on my own in a country where I can't speak a word of German. C'mon now!"

I came to immediately when Monette squeezed my hand so hard I was sure she was going to extract oil from it.

"Robert, c'mon, Robert!" I could now hear her saying through gritted teeth. "I have no idea what's going on, but it doesn't look good. Everyone's standing around me covering their mouths in horror and pointing to you accusingly. C'mon, Robert," she implored.

"What happened?" I asked. "I was having sex with the count upstairs . . . he left me and didn't return. I remember coming down to look for the count because he was pretty drunk at the time . . . and then I went into the lavatory and . . . something about the count having a knife in his back."

"That pretty much sums it up. Robert, I hate to break it to you, but it looks like the count had an accident."

"An accident?"

"Yes, he seems to have fallen on a knife. It's sticking in his back."

"Fallen?" I asked, completely confused.

"Well, sort of fell backward on a knife someone was holding. He's dead, I'm afraid. Oh, and he's slumped over with his head in a toilet."

Monette, never one for dwelling on unpleasant details, subscribed to the theory that it was best to break shocking news to people quickly. In other words, if you hit someone in the face with a shovel quickly enough, they won't really notice it. For example, if someone phoned Monette with the bad news that your aunt was found crushed under a semi filled with kumquats, Monette would interrupt you during dinner at a Mexican restaurant by saying, "I've got to tell you your aunt is now guacamole on Interstate 10 outside Phoenix. Sorry. Now, could you pass me the salsa?"

Having told me the shocking news, she stood there waiting for a reaction from me. A sudden bursting into tears? Tearing my clothes, screaming, "Why? Why?"

But the weirdest thing happened. I didn't cry, yell uncontrollably, or pitch myself off a building roof. Being raised in a family where emotions were roundly suppressed and denied, I took the devastating news rather well. That, coupled with the fact my whole relationship with the count was an unreal fantasy, made his untimely death seem strangely unreal, too. And, in all honesty, the thought that I was probably a very wealthy man did cross my mind a few hundred times.

"Could you help me stand up, Monette? Where's Michael?"

"I haven't seen him all night," Monette replied. "He was hot after some guy covered with scary tattoos and disappeared with him an hour ago."

There was a commotion in the crowd that surrounded me, which parted to admit a large, bear-like man with a red face followed by a band of serious-looking men in green uniforms with the word *polizei* embroidered on them. I still knew very little German, but even a redneck who thought that the Grand Ol' Opry in Tennessee was every bit as good as the Cologne cathedral could guess why they were here—and interested in talking to me. I decided to stand up.

The policemen dressed in green uniforms were actually quite gorgeous, especially their leader. His close-cropped hair, stern square jaw, and ice-blue eyes gave him the look of a hawk in human form. The bear-like man introduced himself as Herr Taucher, homicide.

"I am told you were one of the first to find the body of the count," Herr Taucher said in fairly good English. "Could you tell me what has happened?"

Before I could get a word out of my mouth, Michael magically appeared from nowhere and stood next to the cropped-hair commander, latching on to him faster than an alien attaching itself to Sigourney Weaver.

"My name is Michael Stark, and I'm sure I can be very helpful to you, Officer—no matter what you're looking for," Michael purred.

I sat there, speechless. Michael was just being Michael. He was trying to pick up a *polizei* official while I was up to my lederhosen in trouble.

"There you are, Robert—or should I call you Oral Roberts?" he said, looking around at the *polizei* with a sly smile. "Did you get picked up by the German vice squad?" he laughed. "I'm not surprised, what with you puffing on the count's pink panatela upstairs in that linen closet."

"Michael," I tried to say, but was cut off.

"I can't imagine you having sex with Count von Schmidt in that closet—in fact, I can't imagine you having sex, period—but I guess all those years of celibacy must have turned you into a regular horny toad."

"Michael, I . . ."

"Relax, Robert. I won't tell your friends here you've been

such a sex maniac ever since you started dating the count that you probably scared the bejeezus out of him—which is why I saw him come tearing out of that closet around an hour ago faster than Jerry Falwell leaving a whorehouse with a TV news crew in hot pursuit."

Monette felt it was already too late to speak up, but she did anyway. "Michael, the police are investigating an incident involving the count."

"It's not about all those expensive gifts that the count gave you, is it? Are they stolen? Or is it that phony will where he gives everything to Robert?"

"Michael, please shut up," I said.

"Oh, for God's sake, Robert. These guys can't speak English, so they're not going to understand any of this!"

Herr Taucher, who had been scribbling wildly during Michael's verbal diarrhea attack, leaned toward Michael. "How do you spell 'panatela'?"

Michael, slowly realizing he had been digging me into some sort of unspecified trouble, uttered a simple "oops," then continued without a care. "So what trouble is the count in?" he asked.

Monette decided to act as my spokesperson for the time being. "Michael," she reported, "the count is kind of dead."

"What do you mean, kind of?"

"I meant to say he's dead. With a knife in his back!"

"Wow!" Michael exclaimed while whistling. "You mean, like . . ."

"Yes, like *really* not-breathing-and-bleeding-all-over-the-floor kind of dead! That's why the police—who, by the way, can speak *and* understand English—are standing here asking questions."

"Jesus! Last year I got framed for the murder of my boyfriend, and now this! I guess it's your turn now, Robert," he said, chuckling a bit. I looked at Michael's face and could see it light up, indicating he thought he was about to let loose a revelation equal to the discovery that the earth revolves around the sun. "If the count is dead, then you're a very wealthy man! His will made you his only beneficiary! Congratulations, Robert! You aren't poor anymore!"

I knew then and there that, no matter how dangerous it would have been to open the door of the count's chartered jet in flight from Monte Carlo and push Michael out over the Alps, it was something I just should've done and asked questions later.

"Thank you, Michael, your testimony is just what I needed. Just hand me a blindfold and let me listen for the crack of the rifles."

"Robert, remember, I'm on your side. I'll get you out of prison, don't you worry. I know what I'm doing. I've talked my way out of more speeding tickets than you can imagine."

"*Talked* your way out of speeding tickets?" I asked incredulously. "I'm sure you used your mouth for something, but it wasn't talking that got you out of a jam. Getting back to the subject, I didn't really think I was going to *prison*. But thank you for putting that thought in my mind. Now," I said, looking at Herr Taucher, "whatever I can do to help, please ask."

And he did. I told him the complete story of how I met Siegfreid in New York, our whirlwind affair, the gifts, and I even managed to spill some of the sexual encounters, since they might have relevance in this investigation. The only thing I left out of our sexual escapades was the incident in Berlin where the count pulled out a horse saddle and requested he ride me. No need to tell Herr Taucher that one. (Not even you, dear reader, will know whether I consented.)

Taucher conferred with Herr Bear and his buddies, then barked some orders to the *polizei* that were streaming into the ballroom that I didn't quite understand. Herr Taucher then walked over to one of the stairways and mounted a few steps. He shouted to the crowds first in German, then in English, French, and Italian that he wanted everyone to stay put until they were pulled into groups and questioned by the *polizei*. You could hear the murmur from the crowd that plainly said that they weren't exactly pleased with being held against their will—and without drugs.

"I know this all looks pretty bad, Robert," Monette said, trying to put a better spin on the situation, "but some good came out of this whole mess."

"And what's that?" I asked, not completely agreeing with her sunny take on things.

"I learned how to say 'Where is the nearest lesbian bar and do attractive women frequent it?'"

12

Rapunzel, Rapunzel, Let Down Your Dyed Hair

We were told by Herr Taucher to go back to the count's palace and stay put until further notice. The police would accompany us back, conduct a search of the premises, then let us stay for a few days in the castle until they could figure out what to do with us.

When we arrived back at the palace, we were asked to stay in the cavernous music room on the second floor until the police were satisfied with their search of the house. And not that it meant anything, but guards were posted around the palace, and especially outside our door—to keep the press away, Herr Taucher said. I suspected they were there also to keep us from leaving the premises.

I sat around until it was daybreak reading magazines. Monette was dozing on a large couch by the window and Michael was nervously pacing the floor.

"Jesus, when are they going to finish searching the place so we can get out of here? I feel like Rumplestiltskin trapped in a fairy-tale tower."

"Rapunzel. You're thinking about Rapunzel," I corrected.

"Whatever. I just want to get out and meet some guys while I'm in Berlin."

"Thank you for your genuine concern for the situation I'm in right now. But as for being trapped inside, tell me about it, Michael. I've been to Monte Carlo and Berlin and I haven't seen much more than the inside of this palace."

"The ceilings is more like it," Michael corrected me.

"Right," I said.

I was just beginning to nod off and dream of Russell Crowe when I saw something that caused me to become very much awake. In fact, my eyes opened so wide, my eyeballs almost fell out of their sockets.

"Monette, Michael, come here quickly!" I said, motioning for everyone to come look out of the window.

"Uh-oh!" Monette exclaimed.

"Oh, fuck!" Michael added.

What we were all seeing was a body being carried out of the palace on a stretcher. And I mean a body.

I was the first to speak. "Monette, please tell me it's a German custom to cover living people with a white sheet."

"No, Robert."

As the police were busy loading the body into a waiting ambulance, another car pulled up to the gates of the palace, and a woman got out and approached the police who were posted at the entrance to keep the press at a respectable distance. Cameras flashed like mad as the woman was admitted to the grounds and the palace.

Just when I thought things couldn't get any worse, it did. The woman was Mrs. Stark.

In less than a minute, she appeared at the door to the music room.

"What's the big excitement?" Julia said, thumbing toward the corpse outside and acting as if having bodies on your premises was a normal thing. Considering the accidents that occurred on Julia's doorstep in Newport, maybe it was.

"Count von Schmidt was murdered last night. At a party," Michael said.

"Count von Schmidt, Count von Schmidt," Julia repeated, trying to jog her memory. "Was he married to Princess von Thiessen?"

"No, Mother. Count von Schmidt was Robert's boyfriend. You met him in Monte Carlo."

"Oh, *that* one! Dead, huh? I'm *so* sorry, Robert," she said with the amount of emotion that would make Martha Stewart look like a borderline schizophrenic with Tourette's syndrome.

"Thank you, Julia. It's easier to bear the pain when I know people like you care," I said, wiping the sarcasm that dripped from my lips.

"If you need anything—anything—I'm here," Julia said while searching her purse for nothing in particular.

Monette, who was glued to the window, suddenly shouted, *"That's where I saw him before!"* and strode toward the door the way only a six-foot-four lesbian could. "I need to talk to Herr Taucher immediately! I have information crucial to the murder," she said to the *polizei* at the door. He related this information to another officer, who presently returned with Herr Taucher. Monette told Taucher that she wanted to step into the hall with him to discuss something private. Taucher agreed.

Monette was gone for what seemed like an eternity, but returned in a mere ten minutes.

"Is everything OK, Monette?" I asked when she stepped back into the room, smiling.

"Everything is more than OK. Herr Taucher has agreed to work with me and tell me what his department has uncovered."

"Why ever would he do that?" I asked in disbelief.

"Because I saw him at the party," Monette replied.

"I did too, Monette. I saw him come in with his *polizei* buddies," I added, not knowing what she was trying to get at.

"No, Robert. He was there long before that. Dressed as

the Eiffel Tower. Dress made from the French flag, makeup that wouldn't quit, and topped off with a four-foot wig that had a model of the Eiffel Tower soaring above it all."

"I saw that costume—how could you miss it? So how did you know it was him?"

"I saw him come into the ladies' room when his cell phone went off. He ran in there, scrubbed the makeup off, and probably ran to his car to make a quick change so he could meet his buddies at the gate. That's why his face was so red when he walked in with his department. Practically rubbed off his outer layer of epidermis."

"Whew," I exclaimed. "So he was afraid you'd tell his buddies about his being a cross-dresser?" I surmised.

"That's part of it. What got him really worried was that I would tell his wife."

I couldn't believe it. "His wife?"

"Yes. She's caught him cross-dressing before and she said if she caught him again, he'd be wearing a dress in divorce court."

"So that's what did it, huh?" I asked.

"Well, that and the fact that I also saw him using his tongue to check out the dental work of a very young guy on the dance floor earlier in the evening."

"No!" I said in disbelief.

"Yes!"

"So he's agreed to work with you, huh?"

"Apparently. He's already given me what he knows about the body they just carted out."

"So what did they find?"

"Remember those doors in the basement that were locked?"

"Yes."

"Well, behind them is a stairway that leads to an even lower basement, complete with walk-in freezers put in during the Cold War. I'll give you one guess what was in them."

"A Popsicle? One about six feet high?"

"Right you are, Robert," Monette replied, slapping me on the shoulder for getting the correct answer.

"So who is he?"

"They're not sure yet, but Taucher said he'd let me know when they found out."

Michael, who had been thumbing through the latest issue of *Stern* magazine, had, up to this point, been edging closer to eavesdrop without our knowing. When Monette and I realized what he was doing, we both turned and moved farther away.

"I know this comes at a difficult time for you, Robert," Michael said, trying to convey some sense of concern, "but when are we going to eat?" He then turned toward me and, in a voice low enough that his mother wouldn't hear, said, "I need to take another hit of steroids."

Monette, who naturally took charge in matters of grave importance (probably because Michael couldn't get his mind off sex and I was a nervous wreck), replied like the official spokesperson for Herr Taucher.

"Herr Taucher said they should be through searching the palace within the hour. There are a few rooms they're going to put under lock and key and guard until they can search them with a fine-tooth comb. So soon, we can feel free to mill about the house, but they're asking us to stay in the palace—all of us—for the time being."

We all staked out positions on the oversized couches and napped for some time until we heard a knock on the door. Michael sprang from the sofa and leaped to answer the door so quickly I didn't even have time to *think* about getting up.

Michael opened the door a few inches to ascertain who was knocking. When he could see it was Herr Taucher, I heard Michael say, "Could we go out into the hall? Everyone's sleeping," even though a quick glance around told me no one was.

In a few minutes, Michael sneaked back into the room, all eyes on him.

"It was Herr Tower . . ."

"Taucher," Monette corrected him.

". . . yes, Torcher. He said we can move about the house and enter any room except those with a guard posted at the door."

"It's about time," Julia complained loudly. "I was just about to call the American consulate to protest this unfair and illegal incarceration."

I don't know why Julia would say such a thing. I doubted she would ever stoop to going through legal, diplomatic channels to get what she wanted. Those avenues would be too achingly slow. Why not just place a call to the head of the Stark Pharmaceuticals office in Germany and have several of the guards in the palace disappear from the face of the earth? While she was at it, why not have Herr Taucher demoted to a department that ticketed errant dog walkers for not picking up their doggie deposits? Even more disturbing was the question that had never bothered to get answered in all the commotion of the last few hours: Why was Mrs. Stark here?

I let this question come up at breakfast, which we all headed down to immediately. Fortunately, Helmut needed the money and reported to work, despite hearing about the count's death on the morning news—he figured he would get paid, count or no count.

"So what brings you here to Berlin, Mrs. Stark?" I asked, trying to put her on the spot.

"I thought it would be good for Michael and me to get to know each other better," she said.

Monette looked up from her omelet in shock.

I was pretty surprised by this act of tenderness on Julia's part, too. I would be less surprised if *Will and Grace* closed a deal to play reruns on the Christian Broadcasting Network.

Even Michael looked at her. "Gee, Mother," he started,

"I think that would be a great idea, but can it wait until later this afternoon? I would like to take this walking tour of the historic buildings of Berlin."

Michael taking a walking tour of Berlin? First of all, Michael didn't walk anywhere, anytime, unless he was cruising for sex. When he was back in his beloved Manhattan, he even took cabs to the gym, which was only three blocks away. And second, how could history matter to a man who couldn't even remember who he had sex with the night before? No, Michael was hot to trot and nothing was going to stand in his way—not even his mother, who held the purse strings to his expensive lifestyle.

"If you're going to go off *walking* around," Julia said with complete distaste in her voice, "then I think I'll go down to Potsdam today. I want to see if the Communists have left anything worth seeing in what was once a great town."

"I've heard that Sans Souci, which Frederick II built, is supposed to be quite something," I said. "He'd leave his wife, Charlotte, in the city and go to Sans Souci with his boyfriend. I even hear his royal guard had to be a certain height—for reasons that were never explained," I commented, mentally thumbing my nose at Julia.

"It's a summer house, Robin! I'm sure it's pretty if you like quaint, drafty houses," she said, tossing off one of the great palaces of Europe like it was Section 8 low-income housing. "And what are you two going to do today?"

I wanted to do a little shopping along the Ku'damm, but Monette forcefully answered for the two of us.

"I think Robert and I will stay here and just sit in the gardens and read."

What Monette said and what we did were two different things. In a matter of an hour or so, when everyone else had left the house, Monette and I found ourselves in the basement of the palace, walking through the halls, methodically searching room after room, until we came to one we had been in before.

"Shhh!" I said, motioning to Monette to approach with caution. "There's someone inside. Plus, it sounds like there's a television going. Well, I think this is very weird," I whispered. "Everyone's on the town and Helmut and Karl are accounted for. I think we need to get to the bottom of this," I said, grabbing the knob and flinging the door open.

Inside, on a small bed, was Michael Stark and one of the guards—caught in the middle of a very delicate situation. I hastily closed the door and pushed Monette away.

"What? What did you see, Robert?" Monette speculated.

"Uh, something I didn't want to," I said, turning beet red at the same time. "All will be clear in a moment or two," I said, telling Monette to be patient.

A few minutes later, the door to the room opened and a police guard crept out, his shirt still unbuttoned and the laces from his tactical boots flapping wildly as he walked.

"Michael's in there, I suppose?" Monette correctly guessed.

"What gave you your first clue, Monette? Let's give him another minute to get dressed before we go in."

"Right."

We waited a minute at the door, hearing zippers being zipped and pants tugged on.

"Michael?" I asked. "Are you decent?"

"Am I ever?" came the reply from the other side of the door.

We entered and Michael was slumped on the bed acting as if he had been doing nothing more than crocheting a shawl for his feeble grandmother. The fact that I had caught him playing hide-the-Wiener-schnitzel with an on-duty policeman didn't enter the picture. I had to envy Michael sometimes. He seemed to have no morals and only one purpose in life: pleasing himself. I, on the other hand, waited at the end of the long line of self-indulgence, finding that when I finally got up to the front, the window said *closed* or *come back tomorrow*. Why couldn't I stand up people for dinner dates I had just confirmed, throw tricks out without breakfast, or smash into unattended parked cars with my Range Rover without leaving a note on the victim's windshield containing my phone number? I'll give you one reason: I was too guilt-ridden, too Midwestern, and too Catholic. I had more baggage than American Tourister.

"You never cease to amaze me, Michael. An on-duty cop," I said. "How did you do it? I mean, tell me how you seduce guys the way you do."

"The same way you get people to tell you what's going on in confidential police investigations: blackmail."

Monette looked at Michael in horror. "You didn't!"

"Yup, I told Herr Tobler . . ."

"Taucher," Monette corrected him again.

" . . . yes, Taucher, that he needed to arrange a liaison between me and the hunky cop who was eying me earlier—or maybe Taucher's wife would like to know why those pantyhose she found in the closet never seemed to fit her."

Just what I said. No morals. When it came to getting something he wanted, Michael had no compunction in revealing how he pulled off something completely underhanded. It was almost as if he were proud he'd finally found a use for his mind.

"What *are* you watching?" I asked, looking at the television and seeing a man on the screen sitting in a chair, eating. "And I thought American television was bad."

"This is a videotape, Robert!" Michael said. "I met Rainer here—that was the cop's name—and I thought a little porn would help things along."

"Where was your trusty blindfold and rubber gag?" I asked, knowing all too well the sex toys Michael often employed.

"Can you believe it? I left them at home—and I never travel without them! But, you know, traveling with Mother."

"Traveling with Mother what?"

"I was traveling with my mother during the first part of this trip. Or don't you remember?" Michael asked exasperatedly.

"I remember. But what's that got to do with things?"

"Mother searches all my luggage. She always does. So I couldn't have any sex toys in there."

"She does this whenever you travel together and you think this is normal?"

"Robert, my mother decides in her mind what is normal and I let her think I'm obeying. But she knows I cheat. I knew she'd go through my stuff, so I left a few items in there to show I was a good boy."

"Like what, for instance?" I was intrigued to know what Julia would fall for.

"A Bible. Um, a book . . . *Homosexuality: Myth or Reality?* . . . and a picture of my mother in a silver frame."

Monette was appalled. "And she actually fell for this?"

"We both play a game of constant deception. She lets me know in no uncertain terms she wants a straight, upstanding son and I let her think she has one. But we both know it's all a big lie. As they say, denial isn't just a river in Egypt."

"So you and your friend got aroused by watching a videotape of a man sitting at a table eating?" I asked, squinting my eyes to figure out who the man in the video was.

Michael gave me a surprised look. "Robert, this video is probably hard-core porn compared to the stuff you insert into your video player."

Monette closed in on the TV screen. "My god! It's Siegfreid! Eating!"

"So? I've had dozens of videotapes of me taken before!"

"Yeah, but not of you eating . . . I take that back. Never mind," I finished, realizing that one more word and I would be pulled down into the depths of another Michael Stark depraved sex-ploit.

"I know you're sad and all that, Robert, but this count was a real narcissist. I mean, who would have all these tapes

taken of himself eating, talking on the phone, having cocktails with people? This guy was really stuck on himself!"

I didn't even touch this thought. *Too easy. Just let it go,
Robert.*

Monette stood staring at the TV screen as if in a trance.
"I don't get it. The tapes are black and white and look as if
they were taken with a surveillance camera." She turned to
speak to Michael. "Why did you think they were porn tapes,
Michael?"

"Because of the labels on the side of the videotape boxes.
See, here," Michael stated, grabbing a handful from a shelf.
"Check out these titles: *Flesh Puppets, Berlin Buttboys,
Foreskins Away!*, and *Hot Rods*. Look at the size of the rod on
this one," Michael said, gesturing to the picture on the back
of one of the explicit boxes. "Too big, even for me."

Monette looked away in disgust. "I guess when you have
works of art and live in a palace, you have to have security
cameras everywhere. I wonder if we've been on camera all
along?" she mused.

The look of horror on Michael's face was almost terrifying—but not half as terrifying as the look on *my* face. "Uh-
oh!" I uttered.

"What's the matter?" Monette asked. "It looks like
you've seen Roger Ebert with his clothes off."

"I just had a scary thought—although not quite as scary
as the one you just mentioned. The count and I had sex all
over the house, and it's probably caught on videotape everywhere."

"So you're afraid the police will find the tapes?" Monette
ventured.

"No, I'm afraid they'll see what I did on them."

Monette smiled with that oh-boy-delicious-dirt look. "And
what sort of things did you do on those tapes? You have to
tell me, because I'm on this case and it could be important,"
she said with a naughty chortle.

"Well, Siegfried dressed up like a priest in a latex priest

outfit and I wore a choirboy's outfit—not in latex," I said, as if wearing a choirboy's outfit with a high wool content during a sexual act was acceptable. "And he kind of lit candles in places where candles should never burn," I said, calmly exposing myself to the greatest potential blackmail ever allowed.

Monette stared at me with her mouth open for what seemed like an eternity, so I carefully reached over and gently closed it for her.

When she didn't respond, I ventured even deeper. "Is it the candle thing?"

"No, no, I'm still trying to get past the latex priest thing. Where *do* you get a latex priest outfit? I can't even get jeans to fit me!" she complained.

"Could we leave this conversation . . . and this room?" I pleaded.

"Yes, I think we need to go upstairs and look at some of these hidden cameras. This is just too strange. The footage of Siegfreid in the music room having cocktails with various people intrigues me."

We went upstairs to the music room, went to the bookcase where the hidden camera captured the count and his friends, and guess what we found?

No camera. No wires, either. No holes bored in bookcases.

We went back down to the room where we found the videotapes and checked out the scenes captured in other rooms. Then we went to those rooms and I give you just one guess what we found. If you answered nothing, you just won an all-expenses-paid vacation to Scapoose, Oregon.

"I just don't get it," Monette moaned. "Why would the count have surveillance cameras all over the place and then have them taken out suddenly? I just don't get it."

I began to relax a little—a little, I said. If the cameras looked like they were taken out a while ago, then maybe my little acting debut wasn't caught on tape for all to see. I tried to divert attention elsewhere. "Maybe the count was trying to catch the murderer on tape, blackmailing him or something, and when he got whatever he was after, he had the cameras taken out. I don't get the lack of holes in the cabinetry, though."

Monette, who seemed uniquely stumped until now, seemed to make her first discovery in the case, however small. "Robert, I'm sure there are miniature video camera-recorders that fit inside a book or something. But if what was on the tape was so important, then why stockpile the tapes downstairs in a servant's quarters when you would want them where someone could find them in case you were murdered? I think we need to look at those tapes more closely."

"Do we have to?" Michael whined. "I was thinking of going out for a while."

"Michael, Stevie Wonder could see right through you," Monette stated. "Didn't you just finish having sex a few minutes ago?"

"Yes, but that's ancient history, Monette."

"My god, Michael, you really are a *machine*! Go on . . . go!" she commanded. "Sometimes I wish I had your four-wheel sex drive, Michael. Mine wouldn't even push a tricycle downhill."

"I'll be gone for just a little while," Michael said, leaving Monette and me to investigate our latest clue.

Monette and I took the tapes and went through them together. We started reviewing the tapes at regular speed, but when we discovered how many there were, we decided to fast-forward through them. We watched the count eating alone, yelling at the servants, having cocktails with friends, talking on the phone, reading books and magazines, getting head from a muscular skinhead . . . wait a minute!

"Uh," was all Monette could say.

"Wait a minute. I want to see this," I exclaimed, slowing the tape down to regular speed. I watched as an anonymous gay skinhead wearing a leather collar and army fatigues polished the count's family jewels to an erogenous luster. "Well," I said, trying to be as adult and open-minded as the heir to a shipping fortune could be, "he obviously did this before my time, so I guess this is none of my business. Being a citizen of the world, I have to be open-minded about this sort of thing. I guess that's what it means to be a European." I paused briefly and changed gears. "I'm not sure I minded being an uptight American, though."

Monette looked at me, stunned at what she was seeing. And, as a card-carrying lesbian, revolted—a fact that she made clear to me, punctuated with two fingers being thrust down her throat.

We fast-forwarded the tape again, only to find more and more examples of the count and his unquenchable libido. It was only when I saw the count dressed in a latex priest's outfit that I hit the ceiling.

"That son of a bitch!" I frothed. "He told me I was the only one he had ever played the priest with—he probably meant *that day!*"

"Relax, Robert. Maybe the fact you're fabulously wealthy is some balm for your weary mind. Look at it this way: a hundred million deutsche marks would buy a lot of penicillin."

"Thank you, Monette," I said with complete exasperation. "Now I feel secure in the knowledge I'll be the only millionaire at the VD clinic! So give me your opinion, Monette. Where do we stand? Any theories yet?"

"I don't know. It's too . . . too many loose ends. Too much of this case is too messy. It's too . . . too! In my experience in having read every mystery ever written, murder is never this messy. There's something we're not seeing that pulls this whole thing together. I've got to think," she said, putting her head in her hands like great detectives always did.

"Monette?"

"Yes?"

"Do you think the will is going to hold up in court?"

Monette looked at me and saw exactly what was going through my mind. "You want to be filthy rich, don't you?"

"Wouldn't you want to be?"

"No, Robert. I really enjoy working for the Endangered Herbs Society of America, making thirty-six thousand dollars until I reach the age of sixty-seven, when I can look forward to fabulous meals of Seafood Medley or Fancy Feast eaten right out of the can. Of course it would be nice to know where my next rent check was coming from. Or to be able to go on vacation to somewhere that doesn't include a dysfunctional relative because I can't afford anything better. Do I want to be rich? You betcha!" she said.

"To tell you the truth, yes, a bazillion deutsche marks would make me feel a lot better . . . but I was also thinking it would make it easier to hire a very good German lawyer."

"Believe me, I'll solve this whole mystery or my name isn't k.d. lang."

"So you don't think this case is hopeless, do you, Monette?" I pleaded.

"Oh, no. It's a notch above hopeless," she said, brimming with strained cheerfulness.

A notch above hopeless, I thought. In a nutshell, Monette had just described my life. Well, at least one notch above is one notch up.

13

From Hopeful to Hopeless with Enthusiasm

As the day wore on, Monette and I sat on the couch in the music room and stared at each other without moving. I now knew how Whitney Houston must have felt on her wedding night with Bobby Brown.

While Monette was lost in thought, the phone rang, jarring us back into reality. I answered the phone, found it was Herr Taucher, and handed the phone to Monette.

"So you found out who the body in the fridge was? Uh-huh. Uh-huh. Uh-huh. Um. Yes. Wow! Is that so? Very interesting. Verrrry interesting. Robert? Yes, that was him who answered the phone. OK, I'll tell him. That's right. Let's talk later today. I have a few phone calls to make. *Auf wiedersehen.*"

I was boiling over with excitement until Mrs. Stark entered the room. Monette sounded confident and like she would solve this messy affair soon.

"What did the inspector say, Monette?" I asked impatiently.

"He said you're his prime suspect and within minutes, a *polizei* will be here to confiscate your passport."

My heart broke through my chest as I felt an overwhelming sense of dread only equal to facing Sister Mary Gonzales in third-grade Catholic catechism. (Despite the happy-go-lucky nature she projected to our parents, I still maintain she carried brass knuckles in the pockets of her habit and worked closely with Latin American dictators as a torture expert. You wanted a confession—however false— against a Marxist guerrilla? Call Sister Mary! She can choke a man with her rosary beads or do things with a crucifix that artist Andre Serrano never even contemplated.)

"Well," Julia reported contentedly, "I guess now that The Wall is down, they don't torture prisoners the way they used to, Robert. But I've read that a lot of the old East German secret police, the Stasis, are still around. In fact, a lot of them now work for the German penal system."

"Thank you for the words of positive encouragement and support, Mrs. Stark. Now, if you don't mind, I could use a handful of Seconals."

"I'd glad to help, Robert," Julia said, rushing to my execution. "Not in an overdose, mind you. You just might want one to sleep, what with all that's hanging over your head."

Julia's unusually long emphasis on the word *hanging* was just another salvo in her attempt to inflict further damage. She was obviously angry her attempts on my life at her Newport mansion failed, and if you can't kill 'em, at least wound them.

I've always suspected the American prison system is missing a model employee by not hiring Julia as head executioner. She'd plunge an intravenous needle into the arm of a condemned criminal without a hint of emotion, turn to the assembled, teary-eyed witnesses, and wonder what all the fuss was about.

Monette spoke up. "I wouldn't start ordering prison overalls just yet. Herr Taucher just told me the body found in the house was a customs inspector."

"Customs inspector?" I said, completely baffled. "Do you think he was letting the count ship stuff into the country with a blind eye, then decided to squeal unless the count paid up?" I conjectured proudly, thinking I had single-handedly solved the case.

"Robert, as usual, you are completely wrong. He was a customs official at the airport, assigned to a part of the airport where the smaller jets came into the country. And get this, mostly private jets. His name is . . . was Ralf Reimann."

"Whoa!" I commented.

"It gets even better. After the announcement broke on the television news, several wealthy people came forward and confessed Ralf was shaking them down for money."

"I don't get it," I said.

Monette continued like a bloodhound on the trail of an escaped convict with a body-odor problem.

"The customs guy was blackmailing wealthy German citizens. Ralf would plant contraband in their luggage and then pull them aside and tell them he would let it go, but he'd talk to them later. Naturally, no one wanted a hint of scandal, so they'd pay him off. He didn't ask for a lot, so most people put up the money rather than risk having a lot of publicity."

Things were becoming a little clearer to me. "So do you think he had something on the count, tried to extort money out of him, and Siegfreid lured the customs guy here, killed him, and put him on ice—so to speak?"

"That's certainly a possibility," Monette conjectured. "But it would have to be something really important to kill someone. You don't murder someone because they put a few grams of cocaine into your luggage."

"So you think it was something bigger? Like the count's shipping business?"

"I don't think we know enough yet. But it had to be something that threatened the count enough to commit murder."

"I don't know," Julia spoke up, thumbing through a German equestrian magazine, presumably trying to get in touch with her four-legged relatives. "I think some people deserve to be murdered for reasons others may consider petty."

Like mother, like son. They both seemed to speak without considering the impact of their words. On the other hand, perhaps they did. That was the unnerving thing about Julia: I never knew if she was just a clueless, overly pampered Republican fossil completely uninterested in the less fortunate of the world, or playing an insidious game of cat and mouse. We both chose to ignore her comment.

Julia continued. "Robin, what is the name of the manservant here? I need someone to send my clothes out for dry cleaning."

"Karl," I answered, hoping it would get her off my back and out in front of a fast-moving intercity express train.

"You know, I like that guy. He's helpful, professional—knows what he's doing."

It figured Julia would take a shine to Karl. Like two peas in a pod. Never mind Karl was a homosexual. Julia and Karl were united by another, more intense bond: homicide.

I turned back to Monette. "The one thing that bothers me, Monette, is that Ralf's murder doesn't solve the problem of who killed the count, does it?"

"No, but it means there's another suspect out there."

Julia uttered a quiet tsk-tsk, and her face fell in disappointment that I was no longer the only prime suspect. "Maybe the count killed the customs guy and then the customs union killed the count for revenge. I've heard unions are very strong here."

Monette gave me a when-is-she-going-to-leave look and continued. "There are a few questions to which I want answers. First, why did the count make those videotapes? I mean, who was he trying to catch on tape and why? Second, why did Siegfried kill Ralf—and when? What did the guy have on the count? Third, when the count—in a drunken state—left you in the linen closet, who did he meet along the way before he ended up . . . where, er, he ended up. And fourth . . ." she said, trailing off.

"Yes, Monette?" I asked, trying to coax out what could be a significant question in this inquiry. "The fourth?"

She looked up right into my eyes and spoke. "And fourth, am I the only fucking person who thinks Anne Heche's autobiography, *Call Me Crazy*, is the most understated book title of this century?"

I looked up at Monette and laughed, letting a little stress out of the situation. Julia, however, looked over at me and signaled with that puckered face of hers that jokes about that Ellen Degenerate woman were not amusing. Mrs. Stark probably never forgave Mary McCarthy for injecting lesbianism into her 1963 novel, *The Group*. I mean, why spoil a perfectly good story about a bunch of Vassar girls by acknowledging the dirty secret that some women love women? But you'd think that, judging from the sort of heterosexual men I've seen in monied circles, becoming a lesbian seemed like the only sane choice. Conversely, if Julia represented the typical American heiress, it's a wonder more wealthy men weren't gay.

Shortly after Monette compiled a list of questions she wanted to ask Herr Taucher, she gave him a call.

"Number one, which servant occupied the room where we found the surveillance videotapes of Siegfreid? I see," she said, motioning for me to get her a pen. "The count kept detailed records of his servants? That's certainly good for us, isn't it, Inspector? Uh-huh, you found the records in Siegfreid's papers. Uh-huh. Name? Manfred Weber? Do you know where he's living now? You're looking into it? Good. Oh, when you locate some information about him, could you get me a picture, if that's possible? You can? Good. OK, second question. What about the will Robert gave you, the one where he gets everything? Euw! A forgery. That's bad. The real one was at his lawyer's office in Berlin. And who are the beneficiaries on that one? Yes, I know that's privileged information. No, the information won't leave this room. Uh-huh. Uh-*huh!* Interesting! And who's he? Tell me about him. Yes . . . yes . . . no! Wow! OK, slow down. Uh-huh. You'll find out where this guy lives, right? Good. And the other? Heino? Yes, Robert's met him. I'd like to know more about him. What's his role as business partner? That's a heck of a lot of money to inherit. No one else? No. Well, this is really interesting! OK, third question. Robert says he overheard the count talking to Ludwig Buxtehude on the phone and he heard Siegfreid yelling at Ludwig that he wouldn't give him another penny . . . or deutsche mark or whatever. Could you find out if there were any monetary arrangements between Siegfreid and Ludwig? You know, loans, personal notes, business arrangements, that sort of thing? Yes, thank you. OK, question number four. Siegfreid had a lot of servants working for him before he fired them all. Oh, you are, are you? Well, you're two steps ahead of me! Here's my last question. Did you turn up any information on Siegfreid's art dealer by the name of Uli? You know, the one Robert and Michael saw eating lunch with the count and who later showed up at Robert's going-away party? I guess that will do it for now. Yes, let me know when you find out anything else. OK, *auf wiedersehen.*"

"Monette?"

"Yes, Robert?"

"I think I heard you right when you said the will was a forgery."

"You are correct."

"So I'm not rich?"

"Not even close. The only thing you are right now is in trouble."

"That's what I was afraid of. So who got all the money?"

"Half went to Siegfreid's old lover, a Hans Sattler. The

rest went to Heino, his business partner. And that's it," Monette sighed.

"That's it, huh?"

"Yes, that's it."

"I'm not happy," I reported.

"How do you think I feel?" Monette whined. "I was hoping you'd be a rich widow so you could give Monette, your soul mate and good buddy, a huge chunk of your inheritance."

"I'm tired of playing the widow," I responded. "So you also found out that the servant who had the videotapes in his room was a Man-something."

"Manfred. Manfred Weber. They're going to find him and question him—along with all the other servants. I'm sorry I can't tell you much more right now. But Inspector Taucher said he could have a lot of answers by tomorrow morning. So you'll just have to live with the dread hanging over your head in the morning."

"Morning?" I replied. "The dread will be hanging over my head tonight—Michael's taking me out to a bar."

Much later that night, Michael dragged me out to a bar near the palace. I don't even remember the name, but Michael assured me it translated to "Lick My Boots" or something like that. I was dressed in jeans and a T-shirt. Michael was dressed similarly—that is, until he dragged me into a nearby hotel and up to a room where he pulled out a key and opened the door, telling me to step in for a minute.

"Michael, where the fuck are we, and why are you opening a suitcase and putting on a California Highway Patrol uniform with tall black police boots?"

"This is *my* room, oh limited one!"

"What do you mean your room?"

"Just what I said. You know, Robert, no wonder you always get the short stick in life. You don't know how to think outside the box. You're so Midwestern in your thinking. You need to think like a New Yorker. You know, to be more devious. Whenever I travel with my mother, I always have a second room at another hotel to store my stuff and," he said, moving aside a tub of body lube large enough to indeed be a tub, "I had some of my more incriminating stuff shipped ahead to Monaco, then to here when I knew I was coming this way."

"You didn't want your mother to see you brought your fetish gear, huh?"

"No, but the main reason is this gives me the perfect place to bring my men, without anyone at the palace knowing about it."

I knew the answer to the question I was about to propose, but I had to ask it anyway. "So have things been busy here?"

"More than you will have in a lifetime, Robert. Let me translate: at least a dozen times."

"But the count is barely cold!" I said, completely astounded. "At least a dozen times?"

"The count was not *my* boyfriend, Mr. Count Stealer! And to answer your question, of course I had sex here dozens of times, Robert! But I didn't do them one at a time! I couldn't rack up numbers like that unless I did a few twos and threes. Listen, I wasn't about to sit around that dreary palace all day under my mother's thumb. My motor was running and my wheels needed to hit the pavement!"

"So the *polizei* in the servant's room in the basement wasn't enough for you?"

"One man? You've got to be kidding, Robert! I think in powers of ten when it comes to men. You and Pat Boone must be the only people in America who think monogamy is the answer. Now, would you stop with the questions and help me get these handcuffs into the cuff case on the back of my utility belt?"

"You're going to wear this out to the bar, aren't you?"

"No, Robert, I'm just trying this on in Europe because this outfit needs some taking in and the tailors are so much better here. Of course I'm wearing this! You just watch how many guys will come crawling up to me with this on. Literally."

"I'm sure your family is pretty much used to having people crawling up to them, pleading. Your mother probably enjoys it immensely."

"Oh, shut up, Robert, and let's get going. The night is slipping away."

Michael gathered up his police search gloves and flashlight and hustled me out of the door, through the lobby, and out into the street.

"Michael, people are staring at you."

"Yeah, what about it?" he replied, pulling out a gigantic cigar and lighting it.

"They're probably thinking I'm under arrest from Interpol or something."

"So?" was Michael's reply.

"Well, isn't it illegal to wear a uniform in a foreign country?" I added, worrying I would end up in even more trouble with the *polizei* than I was already. "The police are probably following us right now."

"So?" Michael repeated.

There was no getting through to Michael, so I remained silent—and at least a few paces behind him—on the rest of the walk to the bar.

The bar was situated in a fairly genteel neighborhood and looked quite innocent on the outside. But once you got inside, it looked like a gay steel mill, with perfectly placed metal I-beams and bolts jutting out of walls, presenting handy places to suspend all sorts of items, from slings to handcuffs. Most of the clientele were dressed in typical skinhead outfits: black knee-high boots with white shoelaces, short-sleeved knit shirts that buttoned up like a polo shirt, and tiny suspenders.

"Isn't this a great place?" he said, elbowing me to validate his taste in bars. "Now, I know that from upstairs this place doesn't look like much, but you should see the downstairs. Let me rephrase that: you should feel the downstairs."

"Feel?"

"It's totally dark down there. You just walk around the maze of rooms and people grab you and you can have sex with anyone you like! All the leather bars in Germany are like this. It's great!"

"Michael, you didn't tell me this was a leather bar!" I whispered in a voice that almost shouted.

"What did you think it was with a name like Lick My Boots?"

"I don't know. I thought it might be a country-western bar."

"Robert, I don't think you'll find a lot of gay men two-stepping in Germany. Look, it's not a heavy leather bar, but there are a few guys here who will do things to you you're probably afraid to even fantasize about."

"Michael, getting groped in the basement of a bar is not my idea of a fantasy. Plus," I added, kicking in the side of my mind that spent its days wringing its hands, "did you ever think that these basements are probably horrible fire-traps? I'll bet they don't even have emergency exit lights."

"Robert, only you would put exit signs before a good blow job. Did you want to check the outlets down there to make sure they're properly grounded? Hmm?"

"You can go downstairs, but I think I'll stay up here. I'd leave, but I don't know my way home. I'm afraid I'll take the wrong turn and end up in Poland."

"Fine," Michael replied, rubbing his hands together with delight. "I'll be back in an hour. Have fun!"

"Oh, I'm sure I'm going to have a rockin' good time! Make sure you have some protection," I said, like a good mother would.

"I never go out without condoms."

"I wasn't talking about *that* kind of protection. Judging from this tribe, I'd carry a knife."

"Why don't you break a bottle on the bar counter and stand in a corner, threatening anyone who comes within twenty feet of you? That ought to get you some pretty hot dates."

"Michael, I would think doing so would make me the most popular guy in the place."

"Have it your way," Michael announced, then disappeared into the back of the bar and presumably into the bowels of the building—pun intended.

If it wasn't enough that I was stuck in a foreign country and a prime suspect in the murder of a high-profile gay man with a title, I also found myself standing in a German leather bar without the slightest idea of what to do. So I did what any red-blooded gay man would do: I drank.

As I was standing in the darkest corner I could find near the entrance (for a fast getaway), a handsome man came up to me and said something in German. I answered back in the only complete sentence I could muster: *"Ich sprechen wenig Deutsche."*

"Then it is English that you speak?" the man said. "I speak good English, pretty much so, you see? My name is Christian."

I felt it wasn't worth quarreling with Christian's grammar, since I was happy I could converse with someone here. At least it would make the time go faster until Michael returned.

We struck up a conversation that wobbled and staggered like a drunk on roller skates, with each of us asking the usual bar-talk questions: how do you like living in Germany/the United States, what do you do for a living, is the weather always this beautiful here, and do you live around here? The answers to these questions were pretty mundane, but I wasn't prepared for Christian's response when I told him I was staying at the palace of Count Siegfried von Schmidt.

"He is the dildo up the rear of a much dirty pig, you know!" Christian said, the corners of his mouth turning down in disgust.

I didn't quite know what to say, fearing something had gotten lost in the translation. "I'm sorry, Christian. Could you repeat that?"

"Yes, you can be sure. He is the dildo up the rear of a much dirty pig."

"That's what I thought you said."

Christian took another swig of beer from his glass and scanned the bar for potential dates.

"Christian?"

"Yah?"

"Why is the count like a dirty dildo in a pig?"

"No, I said he is the dildo up the rear of a much dirty pig. It is much different."

Obviously I was missing some subtle spin on the words, but I did at least gather that Christian didn't exactly like the count. "So why is the count such a bad man?" I inquired.

"His head has much shit in it," Christian continued. "He has sex with many men here all the time. One time, he has the sex with me and in morning, he tell me to leave his house with no breakfast. No thank you. Nothing! He sees me in the bar and never talks to me! He is always like that. Ask any man here. He has treated them all like swine."

In order to prove his point, Christian gathered several people he knew and asked them to tell me what a head of shit the count is.

"*Was*," I corrected Christian. "The count is dead. Someone killed him."

"Good! May I know the man who did this? I want to shake the hand of this man!" Christian said, without a shred of remorse. Several of the men standing around listening to Christian nodded their heads in agreement.

Christian told me he was sorry "the count caught you in the web of his sexy fishnets," and excused himself to go cruise a guy with a shaved head and a nose ring that could easily hold a hundred house keys.

I stood there shell-shocked. Obviously, the count was on his best behavior for me, but was completely contemptuous of everyone else. Just as I was about to try and ponder what all of this meant, there was a loud commotion at the back of the bar. Michael came from behind a curtain that obscured the entrance to the basement and hurried to my side. He was followed by a huge queen who was holding out his handcuffed hands and bellowing words of love like the amorous cartoon character Peppy Le Pew hot on the trail of a voluptuous female skunk.

"Where are you, my little Erik Estrada?" the BOQ (Big Old Queen) said, looking all over for Michael, who was cowering behind me. The BOQ soon spotted Michael behind me and was on him faster than a redneck on a six-pack of Budweiser.

The BOQ was none other than Mad Queen Ludwig. Michael had most likely made himself available for anyone who cared to partake of him, and that person just happened to be Ludwig.

"Michael, sir, why did you leave before I was done pleasing you, sir?" Ludwig whined, lifting his still-cuffed hands and running one down inside Michael's shirt and feeling Michael's rock-hard and surgically enhanced pectorals.

"Ludwig, I just had to go . . . to the bathroom," Michael pleaded.

"Then why didn't you come back for me to finish?" Ludwig said as the clatter caused by umpteen necklaces and gold chains could be heard above the thumping German trance music. Also hanging around his neck on a purple chain was a pair of half-moon eyeglasses, presumably used to improve his vision in the dark.

This was too good to be true. Michael's streak of bad dates continued unabated. I decided not to count Michael's encounter with the *polizei* in the basement. I would give that encounter an I for incomplete since Monette and I barged in on that one.

Mad Ludwig went down on his knees and began kissing Michael's boots in a pathetic attempt at eroticism.

"This can't be happening to me, Robert!" Michael said through gritted teeth. "If anyone gets wind of this in New York, I'll be ruined!"

"What happened downstairs?"

"Well, I was standing down there waiting for someone to worship my uniform when out of the blue, I feel this pair of hands on my boots, and before you know it, they were working their way up my legs. I thought it was some hot guy, so I pulled out the cuffs and locked them on him . . . keep licking the boots, Ludwig. Sorry for the interruption, Robert. Where was I? Oh yes, so I shine the flashlight in the guy's face to make him know who was going to be in charge, and what do I see?"

"The Merv Griffin of Germany?" I ventured.

"Worse. Jabba the Hutt . . . with Sarah Coventry jewelry! Listen, Robert, you gotta get me out of this one!"

"Get you out?" I snuffed. "You gotta be kidding me, Michael. As you constantly remind me, I don't have much in the way of standards . . . but at least I wouldn't sink this low."

"This is some kind of curse you put on me. I mean it. My love life has gone to shit ever since you started dating the count. I've had one hateful date after another! Did you put an Estonian curse on me? Please tell me if you did so I can get rid of *this*," he said, pointing to Ludwig still kissing Michael's boots, "so my sex life can return to normal. This is too perverse—even for me!"

"Michael, first of all, the license plate on your car proudly says 'DV8.' There's nothing normal about your sex life. Second, I'm Lithuanian, not Estonian. And third, I have not put a curse on your sex life."

"Well, someone is sending me a lot of bad luck! And Ludwig here is proof of it."

"Yes, it's going to be tough getting rid of him," I consented.

"You have no idea how tough, Robert. I've lost the keys to the cuffs."

14

I'm Just a Prisoner of Love

Michael and I left the bar with Ludwig still handcuffed. I suggested we try to find the equivalent of an all-night German Ace Hardware store for a hacksaw, but Michael had a much simpler solution to our tricky problem: he told Ludwig he wanted him to wear the handcuffs for the next few days to teach him his role as submissive to his master. Plus, Master Stark (or Mr. Chips, as Ludwig took to calling him) was tired and wanted to go to sleep.

This command from Michael produced magical results. Ludwig gleefully licked Michael's boots one more time, then climbed into a cab, holding out his cuffed hands in a gesture of prayer that was, deep down, neither chaste nor pure.

As the cab sped away with Ludwig staring out the back window at Michael and mouthing, "I will serve you, *Meister*," I turned to Michael and said, "You have no intention of ever following up on your promise to Ludwig, do you?"

"About as much chance as Geena Davis being named Best Dressed Woman at the Academy Awards."

"What about the cuffs?"

"He's loaded. He'll find someone to get them off. I've got better things to think about."

"So what's next?" I asked. "We need to figure out a game

plan to this whole murder thing. We need to be logical and stay objective."

"Right. That's why I think that tomorrow morning we need to go see a psychic."

"A psychic? For God's sake, Michael, what good is that going to do us? Actually, I'll go if he can help us out of this mess."

"She! Madame Lola Klingle is a *she*—and one of the most famous psychics in the world!"

"*Lola* Klingle?" I said laughing. I pictured a buxom psychic with flowing blond hair, dressed in a cleavage-showing peasant dress and pouting her lips in a come-hither manner while running her hands seductively over a crystal ball.

"I wouldn't say that if I were you, Robert. Most psychics can hear what people say about them, and the one thing I wouldn't want to do is make a psychic angry."

"You're right, Michael. I wouldn't want her to turn me into a toad or something. "I'm sorry, Lola, wherever you are!" I shouted into the air.

Michael ignored my skepticism and said he would make an appointment for ten a.m.

Michael's actions conclusively proved to me Lola was a fake. After all, if she were so perceptive, wouldn't she *just know* we wanted to see her?

The next morning, I conferred with Monette about where things stood and she brought me up to date.

"It turns out when I called the attractive girl who gave me her business card back at your going-away party in New York, Margaret—that's her name—didn't even know who Siegfreid was. She and everyone there at the party was an actor, hired to act as extras and to fill up the party space."

"Act as extras?" I inquired. "Why would you have a party, then have people for fill-ins?"

"It's done all the time at big New York society parties,

Robert—more often than you realize. People who are unacceptable new money or completely repulsive hire actors to fill in at a party no one in their right mind would show up for. In Margaret's case, they were told to act like the count was well liked and to make the party a success. You know, laugh, cheer, and talk like they were having fun."

"That is too strange!" I replied to Monette's report.

"I think it's the perfect solution the next time you throw a party, Robert. I love you dearly, but your parties are about as dull as watching paint dry."

"When did you find all this out?" I asked.

"I called her late yesterday, so it was early in the morning New York time."

"Monette, while you're waiting for Taucher to get back to you with answers to those questions you posed to him yesterday, why not go with Michael and me to see psychic Madame Lola Klingle?"

"I'd rather have a colonoscopy," she said bluntly.

"Oh, c'mon, Monette. We can both make fun of the zany stuff she says. Please, pretty please?"

"Oh, all right. But I'm not going to let her read the bumps on my head!"

We made a perfunctory attempt to get Julia to go with us, but she planned to spend the entire day shopping and taking advantage of the strong U.S. dollar. The three of us piled into a cab and were driven to a butt-ugly postwar building built in the old East German section of the city. It had all the charm of an electrical transformer station. We battled waves of delinquent teenagers to get from the street to the storefront that held Madame Lola's business, and were greeted by a barking Chihuahua who nipped at my shoelaces ceaselessly. Eventually, a man who wore a stained T-shirt (stained from World World II) and had great tufts of hair sprouting from his ears picked up the offensive canine and tried muzzling it with his hand, but the muffled barks continued from the ill-tempered rat. He quickly, but nonchalantly, ascertained that we spoke English and replied in a voice that reminded me of Boris Badinoff from *Rocky and Bullwinkle* cartoons that Madame Lola would be "shortly out." He then pulled Michael aside so the psychic's world-renowned powers could be amply compensated.

Shortly, a curtain parted in another doorway and out stepped Madame Lola. She looked like a reject from the cast of the *Hungarian Golddiggers of 1923*. She tottered out unsteadily, her carcass desperately grabbing on to any piece of furniture that happened to be within a fourteen-mile radius. She wore mystical robes that looked suspiciously like bed sheets that had been drawn on with magic markers, a turban made from gold lamé, and she had on at least forty pounds of jewelry. I worried that at any minute, I would hear her bones cracking under the enormous weight of her suspect jewels. Even more worrisome than her wardrobe was the stunned look on her face.

"Sit down," Madame Lola's husband instructed us.

"Tell Marlene Dietrich she smells like a fish," Lola uttered as she was carefully lowered into a fold-up chair that had seen both the construction *and* demolition of the Berlin Wall.

Michael looked at the psychic with rapt attention, but Monette and I looked at each other with a mixture of horror, humor, and complete bafflement.

Her husband sensed that instead of giving the impression of being in touch with the other world, Lola clearly showed she had taken up residence there.

He disappeared behind a curtain and quickly reappeared with a strange-looking drinking glass filled with a clear liquid. He explained that the liquid was a magic potion that would help Madame Lola get in touch with the forces of the psychic world, but from my close proximity to her, it smelled amazingly like peppermint schnapps.

The surprising thing was, the drink seemed to focus

Madame Lola's mind so that the more she spoke, the more sense she made—to a point.

"Let us begin," Lola announced.

Her husband, ever the moderator, told Lola Michael was here to have a curse removed from him.

"A curse, a curse, who, who?" she asked.

"This Lithuanian here put it on me," Michael said, pointing in my direction.

"I did not!"

"Someone did," Michael said, always wanting to point the finger of blame in any direction but his own. "I used to have sex all the time and now every guy I drag home is a loser."

I was about to doubt whether Madame Lola would be able to understand—or sympathize with—Michael's predicament, when she spoke up and put my doubts to rest.

"A curse . . . a curse . . . no good. Lithuanians, no good!"

"Hey, wait a minute . . ." I started to say, but was cut off.

"The curse, the curse, gone . . . you must cut, cut, cut, an onion into four pieces, four, four, four, put in the four corners of the building and cover with honey, honey honey."

"Wouldn't that draw ants?" I wondered out loud—a little too out loud.

Lola ignored my comment and proceeded. "Then . . . three eggs, eggs, eggs . . . put in three glasses of water, water, water . . . in one windowsill, windowsill, windowsill . . . in the room where you have sex, sex, sex . . . ."

"Is she kidding?" Monette whispered to me. "Where are we going to get truckloads of eggs delivered to the palace this late in the morning! And what's this about just the eggs? She forgot to add the flour and the salt. Otherwise your popovers won't rise."

This comment caused me to snicker so loudly I had to burst into a coughing fit to disguise my laughter.

". . . after five days," Lola intoned, "pour all out into water far, far, far away from you, you, you."

"Well, I guess that's it!" Michael announced loudly, certain Lola's recipe for bad karma would do the trick. "Robert, since I paid for an hour of psychic time, why don't you ask Madame Lola who killed the count . . . or at least tell her about that dream you told me about, the one with the count dressed as a bishop or something."

"Oh, Michael, I don't think so. I mean, I don't know about that!" I protested.

"You, who mock me last night, calling into air . . . Lola, Lola, wherever you are . . . you mock me . . . you are a bad child!" Lola intoned.

I turned whiter than the Queen of England. How did this woman, who seemed to be oblivious of events in this world, know I was making fun of her last night? Michael must have told her, I reasoned, then crossed myself just to be sure. It couldn't hurt.

"Madame Lola, I'm sorry if I made fun of your . . . awesome powers! Yes, amazing powers. I am but a poor infidel, a skeptic who finds it hard to believe anyone, being raised Catholic. But I am finding out how wrong I am. Please use your powers to tell me," I said, grasping for straws, "what my dream means."

Madame Lola nodded her head, signaling for me to continue.

I told her my dream about finding the count in bed, dressed as a Catholic cardinal and adding great drama to the part where the count chased me through the palace. The only part I left out was the part where Russell Crowe and I made passionate love.

"The count, the count, the count . . ." Lola started. "No cardinal, no cardinal, no cardinal! Not even bishop! No bishop, no bishop, no bishop!"

"If she doesn't stop stuttering in threes, I'm think I'm going to strangle her, strangle her, strangle her," Monette whispered in my ear.

"Costumes, costumes, costumes! All masks, masks,

masks. Too much masquerade, masquerade, masquerade! No more about dream, dream, dream! Next?"

"I was in love with a count. Tell me about him, Madame Lola."

I looked at Monette for approval on my line of questioning. She shrugged her shoulders, figuring why not?

Lola began to moan and weave back and forth in her chair so violently, I worried she was having an epileptic fit.

"You!" She pointed accusingly at me. "Must beware! Beware, beware, beware! Oh, danger, much danger. I feel pain, pain, pain," she chanted.

Pain. The woman feels pain, I thought. *I'm surprised the woman isn't on a morphine drip at her age.* A second thought: maybe she did have an intravenous tube shoved into her arm underneath those robes. That might explain the look on her face.

"I feel a pain in my back, my back, my back! Sharp, sharp, sharp! Cold, cold, cold! Metal, metal, metal. A man, man, man. Near water, water, water. The pain in his back, his back, his back! Drowned, drowned, drowned! I also see a circle of metal, metal, metal! On his head, head, head! Wearing the metal, metal, metal. Ahhhhhhhhhh!" Lola screamed and went limp, her head coming to rest on the velvet tablecloth in front of her.

No one spoke for a while. I looked over at Monette, who, oddly enough, seemed to be in the same trance as the one Lola spent her life in. I tried to shake her awake, but she merely put her arm on mine to stop me and simply said, "Not now. I'm thinking."

Lola's husband, who was waiting in a nearby room, came forth and told us Madame Lola was tired now. Enough.

The three of us got up to go back to the mortal world, yet Monette still looked like we had left her behind in the other.

"What's the matter, Monette? You didn't drink from Lola's glass, did you?" I asked, seriously concerned.

"I don't know—something Madame Lola said. I just can't put my finger on it right now."

"You don't believe there's anything to what she said, do you? She could have read all those details about the count's death in the paper."

"Oh Goddess, no. But she did get me thinking," Monette answered.

"Wasn't she great?" Michael exclaimed. "She knew about the count being stabbed and being found in the toilet, because she said that the man wore metal on his head, a crown obviously and water, drowned," Michael said proudly. "Plus, she kept talking about the masquerade party. The only thing I can't figure out is what she meant about your dream . . . that the cardinal wasn't a cardinal or even a bishop. Maybe she means the count really was a priest after all. There was that latex priest outfit!"

"Michael," I responded, "there's one part of your body that those steroids you're taking isn't helping: your brain. Like your testicles, I think it's shrinking, too."

"Listen, you two," Monette said, breaking her trancelike silence, "I need a little peace and quiet. I'm trying to think."

"Monette, you're not going to take what Lola said seriously, are you? I mean, she could have read all those details in the paper about the count's death."

"Robert, I can't believe you still doubt Madame Lola," Michael interjected. "I would think that she would have made a believer out of you by now. She's one of the world's greatest psychics!"

"How do you know that, Michael? Did that Chihuahua of hers send you telepathic messages?"

"No, it says right here in this guide," he said presenting exhibit A in what Michael figured was an open-and-shut case.

I looked at the guide that Michael thrust in my face. "Michael, this is one of those free, schlocky tour guides they put out to trap unsuspecting Americans into bad restaurants and trashy freak museums. Look at this! Torture museum! Now who in their right mind would go to something like that?" I questioned.

"Hey, I was thinking about checking it out later on this week."

"Michael, I don't think this museum is featuring the kind of stuff you like."

"You never know," Michael replied.

"So you read an ad and believe everything it says?" I continued.

"I do when an advertisement says that Madame Lola predicted the fall of the Berlin Wall and that the former East German communist government did everything they could to suppress her and her psychic powers. They were afraid of her!"

"Michael, I'd be afraid of someone like that running around loose, too."

"Would you two be quiet?" Monette implored us. "I think I'm on the verge of something . . . or maybe it's just a migraine coming on."

So we rode in silence all the way back to the palace, with me looking out the windows of the cab at all of the buildings of Berlin and Michael looking at all the men of Berlin getting away.

When we arrived back within the gates of the palace, Monette went straight to Siegfreid's music room and sat there, staring at where a surveillance camera had previously been placed. Michael came and sat with us, thumbing through another stack of German magazines, "to see if he was making headlines in Germany" as he told us.

"What was the count trying to get on videotape?" Monette wondered aloud. Her face then lit up like a Christmas tree. "Maybe I've been looking at this the wrong way around! Yes! That's it! Someone else was taping the count, trying to catch him doing something illegal . . . to blackmail him."

Two could play at this detective game. "Ludwig and an accomplice?" I suggested. "Remember, I overheard him begging the count for more money and Siegfreid wouldn't give it to him. So he got a friend inside the palace working as a servant who then put the secret videotaping equipment in place to catch Siegfreid doing something or meeting with someone that could be used to blackmail the count into forking over more money."

"The same scenario could have been used by the customs inspector, Ralf," Monette ventured. "Well, I guess that's less possible. I think that Ralf already had something on the count from something he put in Siegfreid's luggage, so why try and blackmail him further with videotapes? The list of suspects keeps getting longer the more we find out."

"Considering so many guys in the leather bar hated Siegfreid's guts, it could have been any number of them who wanted to kill the count," I added. "And I'll bet that a lot of other people around town didn't care too much for him, either."

"Wait a minute!" she said, her eyes opening wide with discovery.

"What is it?"

"Oh, nothing. I thought I was on to something, but it slipped away. Where were we? Oh yes, Ralf, the customs guy. Well, just because people hated Siegfreid doesn't explain why the customs guy ended up frozen in the basement. It looks like the count, or he and a friend, killed the customs guy, and then someone killed the count in retribution. Maybe that's what happened, and the count's accomplice turned on Siegfreid and killed him because he didn't want to split the take."

"The take? What take?" I asked.

"Money, I suppose. Money is the main reason most people commit murder. The second is for revenge. The third reason is family."

"Family?" I asked.

"It's a good reason if you have a family like mine," Monette answered with brutal honesty. She looked lost in thought for a moment. Then her face brightened. "You know what we need?"

"What?"

"We need someone who knew Siegfreid."

"But who could we talk to? We could ask Herr Taucher, I suppose," I suggested.

"No," Monette said, steering in another direction. "We need someone who knew all the dirt."

"I still don't know who we can ask. Siegfreid didn't exactly introduce me to all his friends. Plus, it didn't look like he had a lot of friends."

"Judging from the buzz around town, I'm not sure that he had any. No, we need someone who not only had a lot of dirt on Siegfreid, but is willing to tell all."

"Willing?" I asked.

"OK, busting to tell."

"What about bitchy?"

"Certainly. Bitchy helps," she said.

"Needy?"

"Oh yes, needy goes without saying," Monette answered, finally catching on to where I was going.

"Outrageous?"

"The more the better."

"Desperate?"

"Absolutely."

"Mad?"

"Ludwig!" Monette exclaimed.

While Monette and I smiled at the ingenuity of our plan, Michael looked up from his magazine as if something was haunting him. In this case, it was about to be what happened the previous night in the downstairs of a certain leather bar.

15

I Won't Speak Ill of the Dead, But . . .

Monette called Herr Taucher to invite him to listen in on Ludwig's testimony and get an update on what his department had turned up. Fortunately, there was plenty. Taucher reported that they didn't find anything unusual about Siegfreid's trip to New York—the hotels where he stayed and the restaurants where he ate reported nothing out of the ordinary. But there was one interesting discovery: Siegfreid's former lover, Hans Sattler, had been in New York about the same time the count was.

Siegfreid's business here in Germany was anything but ordinary. Taucher wouldn't give any specific details, but he did reveal Siegfreid's shipping line was under heavy surveillance for smuggling. Of what, Taucher wouldn't say. Even more interesting was the fact that Heino, Siegfreid's business partner (and heir to half of Siegfreid's fortune), was up to his pretty little neck in illegal shipments of some sort.

Many of the former servants had been contacted, and they reported nothing out of the ordinary as far as visitors to the palace were concerned: Heino, Ludwig, Uli the art dealer, and a host of tricks he paraded into the palace and barely escorted out the next morning. The majority of them said they were surprised when they were fired and even more surprised when he gave them all good letters of reference.

As far as Ludwig went, it was impossible to ascertain the state of his personal finances because of strict privacy laws, but no financial connection could be found between Count Siegfreid von Schmidt and Ludwig Buxtehude.

Manfred Weber, the servant who lived in the room where the videotapes were found, still couldn't be located, but did have one interesting characteristic about him: he had a criminal record. No serious crimes, but fraud and trafficking in stolen goods. And Uli, the count's art dealer? Taucher and his staff couldn't find anyone by that name connected to Siegfreid. Finally, several people at Ludwig's ball noticed that a man dressed like the count was seen staggering into the bathroom, helped by another unidentified person.

"Don't you worry your pretty little head, Robert," Monette reassured me. "I think Ludwig will tell more than I think he knows. That's what I'm counting on." She nodded to Inspector Taucher, who was seated quietly in a over-stuffed chair near the windows.

"I hope that what he knows is the truth. If he's as mad as they say he is, I don't know how we're going to rely on what he tells us. Someone at his ball told me that three months ago he rode a horse naked down the Friedrichstrasse in Berlin, claiming he was Frau Godiva."

"Well, we're about to find out," Monette reported as she looked out the window toward the front courtyard. "A car just pulled into the drive . . . and . . . and . . . oh shit, I don't believe this!" Monette said, erupting in a storm of laughter.

"What? What?" I begged.

"Oh Goddess, it's too funny," Monette managed to get out before another flood of laughter unleashed itself in a torrent that ended with me hitting her on the back when something went down her esophagus the wrong way.

Michael, who had tried to bolt the palace when he found

out Ludwig was coming over, was cajoled into staying by pleas that it was necessary to help me out of a jam. He stayed only on the condition his mother would not be allowed into the same room or be told what his connection to Ludwig was.

In a moment, Karl knocked on the music room door and announced her highness. Ludwig, ever the drama queen, sauntered into the room, his hands still cuffed. Taucher raised his eyebrows in amusement, but said nothing. After all, he seemed to be letting Monette run the show. Ludwig walked over to Michael and got on his knees in front of him, causing Michael to turn red with embarrassment I think for the first time in his life. After all, when you're a rich, narcissistic sociopath, you really can't be embarrassed, because it's impossible that you could ever do something wrong or foolish.

"Uh, you can get up now, *sklave!*" Michael said.

I just had to ask. "*Sklave?* What's *sklave*, Michael?"

"Slave."

Leave it to Michael. He couldn't speak a word of German, even refused to learn the basics I tried to teach him, but the one word he picks up and uses fluently is "slave."

Monette, still stifling laughs, began. "Ludwig, thank you so much for coming to talk to us. We are trying to learn more about who may have been involved in Siegfried's death. So the more you tell us what you know about Siegfried and his friends, the easier our job. Do you understand, Ludwig?"

"Oh yes, I understand very much, Motet!"

"Monette."

"Yah . . . Monette."

"Ludwig?" Monette ventured further. "You can take those handcuffs off if you want to be more comfortable," she added.

"Oh no, I can not take these off from mine hands unless the *meister* Stark, he says so."

"Michael, could you take these off of Ludwig?" she inquired.

"No, I can't," was Michael's reply.

"Michael dear, could I speak to you in private for a second?" she asked, beckoning with her curled index finger.

There was a brief, low-volume conference between Michael and Monette that was difficult to hear, but I did manage to catch the phrases "don't know the fuck where the key is" and "don't give a rat's ass what happens to the big ol' queen."

I hoped Ludwig's command of the English language was, like his propensity to go nude, limited. The terse and agitated conversation continued back and forth for some time, until Monette grabbed Michael by the neck in a lesbian death grip I had once seen her use on an anti-abortion protester. This protester made the mistake of blocking her from entering a family planning clinic where a good friend of hers was in dire medical need. There are two things you don't fool around with: God, and an angry Irish six-foot-four lesbian whose patience has just about run out.

"Ludwig?" Dominatrix Monette instructed her *sklave*. "Your *meister* commands you to tell us everything you know about Siegfreid. And if you don't, he will take the cuffs off."

These words had a dramatic effect on Ludwig, who was fidgeting and smoothing the creases on his caftan with the neurotic intensity of a hyperactive child with a caffeine addiction. He immediately stopped moving and looked with humble eyes at Monette.

"Now, Ludwig, tell us about Siegfreid. And you must tell us everything and be truthful."

Ludwig began. "The count, he and I know each other many years, but we are not *best* friends. He is strange man, a, how do you say?"

"Aloof?" I suggested. "Sex-crazed?"

"No, he is a bitch!" Ludwig said happily, now that he had

come up with the right word. "The men of Berlin do not like him."

"Why?" Monette asked.

"I tell you just now. He is a bitch. The men, they are like shit to him," Ludwig said, wiping imaginary dog doo off the bottom of an embroidered slipper for emphasis.

"Michael," I said, "were you and Siegfreid twins separated at birth?"

"Very funny, Robert."

"Ludwig?" I asked, interrupting Monette's proceedings. "Why didn't you tell me Siegfreid was not a nice man when I asked you about him the first time you came to the house, about a week before your ball?"

"I do not know you well. Plus, you have the stars in your eyes about the count. I do not want to tell bad things about people."

"Ludwig," Monette probed further, "do you think anyone hated the count enough to kill him?"

"Well, it is not only men he sleeps with that he treat badly. Workmen, gardeners, cooks, chefs. People tell to me that he dis . . . dis . . . dismissing his servants just a month ago. He is a strange man, but he has acted much strange lately."

"Strange? What do you mean strange?"

"No one see him much a few months ago. He comes and goes, but not so much. He does not eat out much, he does not have sex in the bars much, too."

"Ludwig, who are the count's closest friends? His best friends."

"Hmm." Ludwig collected his thoughts. "Difficult for Ludwig to say, for I do not know him too well. I am good friend, very good, but I never know all of him. He has very little friends. Heino is a friend."

"Did he have a boyfriend after his last one, Hans Sattler?" Monette asked.

"I do not understand."

"After the count and Hans were no longer boyfriends, did Siegfreid have a boyfriend before he met Robert in the United States?"

"I am not sure. I have not seen him much. He could have a boyfriend that no person knows about. He was always good at making secrets. But yah, the count, he has no problem showing his boy sex tricks to others. It is the boyfriends he hides."

"Ludwig, do you remember if Hans Sattler was at your ball?"

"No, Siegfreid would not like it. What is more, I do not know where he live or even what he look like. I think he moved to another city a year ago."

Monette tried a different tack. "Did you borrow money from Siegfreid for any reason, Ludwig?"

All eyes fell on Ludwig, and what they saw was a man trying to cover something up.

Ludwig screwed up his face to make it look like he was scanning a ledger in his brain, then answered unconvincingly, "No. I do not need money, for I have much of it."

"Forgive me for saying this, Ludwig, but you *do* spend a lot of money on clothes, your palace, the grounds, and on parties. This must be very expensive!"

"I have much money. Very much."

"OK, Ludwig, enough of that. Let me ask a different question. When you entered the bathroom at your masquerade ball and found Siegfreid, what did you see when you first walked in there?"

"I had much to drink that night, so I go into bathroom to pee. I have to lift up my dress to pee, so I do. Then I see in mirror the feet. A man's feet."

"Sticking out of the stall," Monette clarified.

"Yes, they stick out and I think this man, he is sick. I must go see. I open door and see Siegfreid."

"Did you see anyone else? Either coming out of the bathroom or going in?"

"No, I see no one. Many people go in there after I scream, but I remember no one in there when Ludwig is in there."

I had no idea what Monette was searching for, but she took a deep breath and let it out slowly, signifying she was done. "Ludwig, I think that will be all. Michael has released you to go. *Now go!*" she yelled, as Ludwig grabbed his handbag and scampered out of the room.

I was completely baffled. "So, Monette, are we getting any closer? I don't see how you got anything out of Ludwig at all. He merely told the same story all along. There didn't seem to be anything new. The main theme seems to be that everyone thinks the count was a prick."

"That *is* the answer. It's been right in front of us all along. Over and over again. We were just too blind to see it!"

I almost went through the floor. "Monette! You did it again! Spill it!" I implored her.

"Not quite yet. There are a few things we must discuss with Inspector Taucher first," Monette reported as the Inspector drew nearer—along with Michael. "Michael?"

"Yes, Monette?"

"You can go now. We don't need your help anymore."

"But I don't want to go! It seems like it's getting real good about now."

"Go, before I call Ludwig back here and tell him you want him as a twenty-four/seven slave."

Three pairs of eyes watched as Michael reluctantly left the room and closed the door behind him.

"You can go downstairs now, Michael!" Monette shouted through the closed door. "I can see you through the keyhole."

As soon as we were certain that Michael had left—a fact

he announced by slamming a door downstairs so loudly it briefly shook the house—we began conferring.

"So, Inspector Taucher, what did your people turn up?" Monette said, rubbing her hands together with anticipation. "Oh, before we begin, I want to thank you for doing so much work on this case. I can't speak the language, so I'm already at a disadvantage."

"Not at all, Monette. You have a very good head for murder. I wasn't so sure about revealing all this information to you at first."

"Well, I *did* make an offer you couldn't refuse."

"I think we understand each other very well. I think you would make a very good inspector of homicide. It is a loss to the world you didn't become a police detective."

"Thank you, Herr Taucher. OK, show us what marvelous information you've gathered!"

"To begin, Ralf Reimann, the customs inspector at the airport, had no known connection to the art world. This was something that concerned me, that Uli Steben and Siegfreid were smuggling works of art in and out of Germany and that Ralf was a part of this operation. I think Ralf may have discovered the count smuggling some art in his luggage and he used this knowledge for purposes of blackmail. Judging from the coroner's report, Ralf was killed somewhere around the time of the second day the count was in Monte Carlo with Robert here. So there was an accomplice staying in the house who probably killed Ralf. The only live-in servant, Karl, took a short vacation in Cologne, but—you must hear this—we discovered he purchased a return train ticket and returned to Siegfreid's house early on Thursday, the day we think Ralf was murdered here."

"He may have returned to Berlin on Wednesday night, but how do you know he came here?" Monette asked for clarification.

"Because he has no other place to live but here in Siegfreid's house, and a neighbor across the street saw him arrive at the house in a cab."

"Well, that is very interesting! Especially since he failed to mention this fact to us. I wonder, why is he hiding the fact that he came back to the house and stayed here while Siegfreid and Robert were in Monte Carlo? Why did he end his vacation early when he didn't have to?"

While we pondered this turn of events, the inspector continued, "Another thing. We discovered Siegfreid's last lover, Hans Sattler, does have a large apartment here in Berlin, although he lists his home in Düsseldorf as his primary residence. He works for a clothing designer in Düsseldorf and travels all over the world—including Berlin quite often, so his apartment seems appropriate."

"Did you find information about any financial deals between Ludwig and Count von Schmidt?" Monette asked, jumping ahead.

"No. Not a thing. It does not mean there are none. Ludwig Buxtehude and the count are very smart people with money, so there are ways of disguising ownership and, to some extent, the movement of money."

Monette had a look on her face that said she was going to spring the big question. And she did. "OK, Herr Taucher. Please tell me you found something about Manfred, the guy who worked as a servant in the count's house and lived in the room where we found the surveillance videotapes of the count."

"I have indeed!" the Inspector announced, which actually sent all six-feet-four of Monette jumping into the air with delight. "I have found out he is living here in Berlin, over in the old East German section. As a criminal with a record, he must keep us informed of his whereabouts."

"And I assume you have checked on him."

"We had someone visit his apartment, but his landlady

said he has not been there much lately. Oh, I have a picture of him . . . from his, uh, mug shot as you say in the United States. It was taken at the time of his last arrest, two years ago." He handed the picture to Monette, who studied it for God knew what.

"What is all this information on the side of the photo?" Monette asked.

"Physical information. Height, weight, eye color, hair color, criminal record," the Inspector replied.

"Could you translate for me, Herr Taucher?" she asked.

"Height, 183 centimeters; weight, 86 kilograms; eyes, green; hair color, blond."

"Nothing out of the ordinary there?" I added, finally speaking up.

"Nothing is ordinary about this case," Monette retorted. "Oh, I have one last question for you, Herr Taucher. Give me the answer to this one question, and I will give you your murderer."

Both Herr Taucher and I looked at Monette with bulging eyes, wondering at how quickly she had come to this conclusion.

Monette continued. "You can't seem to find a financial arrangement between Ludwig and Siegfreid, but you must tell me whether Ludwig is in personal financial trouble right now. Does he have a lot of unpaid debts?"

"So you think you know who did it?" I asked, my heart beginning to race inside my chest.

"I don't think, I *know*," she said smugly. "Well, I'm almost sure. The Inspector's response to my last question will answer everything."

"Then tell us, for God's sake," I commanded her.

" I can't, for two reasons."

"And they are?"

"One, I need to confirm a few things. I need to be sure."

"And the other?"

"It would ruin the effect. I've always wanted to expose the culprit while all the suspects sit around a table and squirm like worms. That's what we're going to do. Oh, and I want a storm with lots of thunder and lightning. And guess what? I've checked the weather for tomorrow night and it looks like we're in luck!"

16

Agatha Christie Who?

I spent the rest of the day reading while Monette sat in the music room with dozens of legal pads, covering them with notes and incomprehensible diagrams, presumably representing suspects, motives, and their relationships to each other. Every once in a while, she would call Inspector Taucher to discuss a clue or gauge the progress of her plan for the next night's "festivities." Monette didn't tell me much about her plans, but she did say Taucher had promised everyone who needed to be there would be there.

That night, Monette and I helped ourselves to the local cuisine, Michael helped himself to the local men, and Julia was having dinner with some couple who "shared mutual interests"—which I assumed were antique furniture, decimating social opponents, and murdering without getting caught. After dinner, Monette and I went out for a few beers and laughed ourselves silly.

The next day, I was too nervous to do much of anything, so I tried to read, then gave up. I settled for sitting out in the garden with Monette, drinking beer and helping ourselves to the appetizers and cunning little sandwiches Helmut brought us throughout the day. I suggested we make good use of Helmut's cooking talents, since after tonight he might be in prison on a murder charge.

"Mightn't he?"

"Mightn't he what?" Monette asked with eyes closed, enjoying the sun passing back and forth across her face as the branches shimmered above us in the increasing winds.

"Helmut might be in prison after tonight. Right?"

"Maybe he will, Robert, maybe he won't," she replied, making no commitment whatsoever.

"Well, then I'd better have Karl tell me where things are around the house in case the police drag him off tonight."

No response.

"I said, I'd better have Karl tell me where things are around the house in case the police drag him off tonight!"

Still no response.

"You're just going to ignore me, aren't you?" I commented.

"What gave you your first clue?"

"The cold, stony silence and the fact you just grabbed your glass of beer and downed the entire contents without taking a breath."

"You know, Robert, you're really developing the mind of a great detective."

"Well, I'm using my powers of deduction right now and I'm sensing there is heavy sarcasm afoot."

"Oh really, Robert? And what else do you sense?"

"I sense you're dying to hear my theory of who killed who and what really happened here."

"I was about to tell you your senses have deserted you, but your sarcasm antenna would pick up on that. But, as to your theory, I am not dying to hear it. I think the more correct phrase is that you're dying to tell it."

"Can I?" I pleaded. "Can I, can I, can I?"

"Fine."

"Okay, I think Siegfreid was smuggling art or diamonds or something along with Uli What's-His-Name, the count's elusive art dealer. When we came through customs, Ralf found whatever it was in Siegfreid's luggage and used the knowledge of what he found to blackmail Siegfreid. Heino is involved somehow in this whole smuggling thing, and while Siegfreid and I were in Monte Carlo, Heino met Ralf in the deserted house and killed him, putting him in the freezer downstairs. Then, with a murder under his belt and the possibility of inheriting all of Siegfreid's money, Heino murdered the count at Ludwig's ball and now he's set for life. The end."

"What about the conversation you heard Siegfreid have with Ludwig on the phone—the one about not giving Ludwig another penny?" Monette posed.

"I don't know. I guess he's wrapped up in all of this, too. He's probably running out of money and borrowed from the count so people wouldn't know he's almost broke."

"OK, now I have a question that will test your theory."

"Let me hear it, Monette."

"If you're going to kill some customs officer in your house, why put his body in a freezer in the basement? Wouldn't you want to get the body out of there? I mean, someone was bound to find it someday and start putting two and two together and eventually end up with four."

"I don't have an answer for that one, Monette. I guess I'll never be admitted to the Hardy Boys Detective School."

"Oh, I'll bet you wished you were running around with the Hardy Boys when you were young. Let me guess, you were in love with Joe Hardy."

"No, Frank."

"Let me make one more guess. You dreamed of going snooping with him and getting into all sorts of predicaments."

My face tried not to show my real thoughts, but Monette read them. She looked at me with a wry smile. "You wanted to be caught by a criminal and get tied up with Frank. I always thought you were kinkier than you let on."

This time, no response from me.

Finally, I spoke up. "I just hope those surveillance cameras in the house weren't operating while Siegfreid and I were here. I don't want to be seen wearing a horse saddle." (There, dear readers—I told you!) "Could we change the subject?"

"Sure. Change it."

"So how close is my theory to what happened? Do I get a gold star?"

"I can't say whether you'll get a gold star, but you will get what's coming to you."

I considered Monette's statement for a moment and then chose my words very carefully before I spoke. "That's exactly what I'm afraid of."

As much as I want to say it was a dark and stormy night— which it looked like it was going to be—there was a more appropriate way to describe it. There is an old Lithuanian saying that it was like a handful of diamonds in a shovel full of shit. Translated: you have to dig through a lot of crap to get to the real gems. Overall, a good saying, however unpleasant the imagery.

This was one of those nights.

Monette had called for everyone to be present at eight P.M. When I joined her in the music room, she was moving about, whistling cheerfully, drawing the curtains and lighting candles.

"Monette, is any of this necessary?" I asked.

"Oh yes. Quite. I've read every mystery ever written, and I've always wanted to do this. So if you want to know who the murderer is, you're going to have to play the game my way," she said. "Now, could you hand me that Ouija board, Robert?"

"Did you want me to go out and rent some wolves so they can sit outside the palace and bay at the moon?"

"I said it before and I'll say it again, I'm going to have some fun with this. I solved this goddamned murder—with the help of Inspector Taucher—and I'm going to expose the killer my own way."

"So you're not going to tell me who did it?" I begged for the umpteenth time.

"Now, Robert, don't you want to have a little fun?" she asked. "You're always saying your life is dull."

"Yes, but sitting next to a murderer is not my idea of a wacky and woolly evening."

"Don't worry, Robert. I'll have several policemen standing guard."

"That's not going to stop the murderer from putting a poison tablet in my drink."

"You know, I didn't think of that! But I do want you to wear a bulletproof vest tonight, just in case a hand slips out from behind the curtain and throws a Chinese jade sacrificial knife into your back."

"Don't joke. I'm worried. And I would feel so much more comfortable if I knew who killed Siegfreid."

"Robert, who do you take me for? This is Monette. Monette O'Reilley. I told you I wasn't going to tell you until it's time. For once in your life, relax! I told you to let it flow with the count, and you went off and had a great time! See?"

"Yeah, and I ended up in the midst—no, make that a prime suspect in the murder of a highly visible gay persona."

"Robert, stop being so pessimistic! You still had the time of your life . . . and the sex of your life. Look at the bright side."

"Monette, when you say that I can't help but think of the end of Monty Python's *Life of Brian*, where the characters are all crucified and they're singing that song, *Always Look on the Bright Side of Life*."

"Well, I for one intend to crucify someone tonight."

There was a knock at the door, and Michael entered with his mother.

"Is this where the party is?" Michael asked.

"I would like to have a cocktail, Robin," Julia asked me.

Like mother, like son. Cocktails are the lubricants that relieve the friction in the Stark family relationships. Michael, who has lived in denial longer than he has in New York City, has maintained his family is very close. To which I respond, yes, but only because it puts them within striking distance. What Michael doesn't realize is that the only things that hold his entire hateful family together are alcohol and a substantial inheritance.

"Julie," Monette said, deliberately mispronouncing Julia's name in an apparent tit-for-tat reprisal, "the cocktails are over there on the sideboard. Feel free to make yourself one," she said, knowing full well Julia would prefer someone from a lower tax bracket do it for her.

There was the sound of a doorbell downstairs and restrained conversation as people climbed the stairs and entered the room, with Herr Taucher leading the pack.

"Is this everyone, Heinz?" Monette asked of Herr Taucher, giving us our first exposure to the inspector's first name.

"This is everyone. Except one. He will be joining us later."

Monette clapped her hands, cracked her knuckles with a nauseating series of popping tendons, and motioned for everyone to sit down at the large table. I couldn't get my mind off the fact that one of the occupants of this table was a treacherous murderer. I looked around the table and recognized the majority of the people there—all men.

"OK," Monette began, "my name is Monette and I will be your host for tonight's murder—well, hopefully there won't be a murder. And to make sure, as you will look around, you will see Herr Taucher is armed, and there are several *polizei* downstairs. I am told you all speak fairly good English, but if there is something you don't understand, please ask me. Now, let's begin. All of you were brought here tonight because you were all friends of the late Count Siegfreid von Schmidt. I will introduce you all around the table. To my right is Michael Stark, present at Ludwig's party; his mother, Julia; Robert Willsop, the last man to see the count alive; Uli Steben, the count's art dealer; Ludwig Buxtehude, at whose party the count was murdered; Heino Schulte, Siegfreid's business manager; Karl Dressen, the count's personal valet; and Helmut Heiting, Siegfreid's personal cook. Thank you for coming. This won't take long."

Monette looked up toward the ceiling, composing her thoughts for a moment, then spoke.

"The murder of Siegfreid von Schmidt began long ago and took a lot of work to make it happen. And it all began in New York City. A young and very naive man living there meets the count. That boy's name is Robert, the man you see here before you. They fall in love, and are soon seen everywhere . . ."

All eyes in the room were suddenly on me. The accusing looks from the faces in the room made me feel like I had killed the count. The voices of guilt in my head told me I had and I didn't even know it! I was just about to confess to the whole thing when Monette continued.

"The count asks Robert to move with him to Germany, and he does. The count is so in love with Robert that the count made out a will giving everything to him—or so Mr. Willsop says. The count and Robert attend Ludwig's masquerade ball and, presto, Siegfreid is found dead and the last person to see Siegfreid alive is Mr. Willsop. So I ask myself, this is all too easy! It looks like this young American has killed the count in order to inherit all of Siegfreid's money. The problem is, the count also kept a will at his lawyer's office here in Berlin. So a handwriting expert looked at the will Robert said was signed by the count."

Michael raised his hand, asking for permission. Monette had no choice but to honor Michael's effort to contribute something to this case.

"It wasn't signed by the count!" Michael said in triumph, thinking only he had come to a conclusion even Pamela Anderson could see coming.

"Thank you, Michael. You're a regular Agatha Christie."

I kid you not, this is what Michael responded: "Agatha Kirsty who?"

"Never mind, Michael. Yes, the handwriting expert tells me the will is a fake. The count's signature is not the handwriting of the count at all! It is close, but not close enough. So something tells me that this young and naive American killed the count in order to get his money. Sometimes these murderers are not as complicated as they may seem. Yes, Robert Willsop, you killed the count in order to become a rich man!" Monette said, raising her voice so dramatically, I was almost tempted to applaud. I wondered what surprise she was going to spring next. But she said nothing. The silence was deafening and the weight of almost a dozen pairs of eyes weighed on my underdeveloped shoulders like a pair of ninety-pound barbells.

"Well, Monette, you certainly had us all fooled. Now I'm sure you're going to tell everyone here that I didn't do it, heh, heh, heh," I said, a lump in my throat the size of a bowling ball.

"I can't change the truth, Robert. Herr Taucher, I think you have your man. Take him away."

I sat there stunned for what seemed like an eternity. I didn't know if I should make a break for it or not, but decided it would not look good. But then again, I started thinking about what life in prison would be like and came to the conclusion it would not be pretty, either. I would make a break for it and jump through the window and fall two stories, landing on my feet like a cat. I would scale the fence like a spider and run to safety right under the noses of the stunned *polizei*.

Then I would go to an Internet café and secure a fake passport, have plastic surgery done on my face to make me look like George Clooney, and go undercover for the rest of my life. Of course, I would also have to have surgery done on my fingerprints so that Interpol, who would have an all-points bulletin out on me, would always be two steps behind me. All their high-tech gadgetry would be no match for my stunningly agile and cunning supermind.

I would work in a used-record store by day, and at night and on my days off, I would search for the one-armed killer who framed me for Siegfreid's murder. I was just about to think how I would use parts from an old radio and hair dryer to fashion into a eavesdropping device ... when a policeman clicked handcuffs on my wrists and led me out of the room.

I wanted to go kicking and screaming, but thought that this would be too undignified, so I simply walked with my head down. Wasn't someone supposed to throw a jacket over my head to protect my identity from the prying press?

This couldn't be happening! Monette, my closest friend, had betrayed me. I was used to Michael betraying me frequently, but this was all a part of his character that Michael said made him so complex and a challenge to understand and love.

As I walked in sheer terror and full of unnecessary guilt, I began to wonder if it would be difficult to play a practical joke on Monette from prison in order to get revenge. Revenge, as they say, is a dish best served cold, but I think my version would involve scarring acid.

I was in too much shock to think clearly, so when the police led me to a room next door to the music room and not downstairs and into a waiting squad car, I didn't quite comprehend what was happening. Were they going to question me there? Were they going to put me in an orange jumpsuit, my new prison wardrobe? Were they going to beat me in order to extract a confession? And most importantly, why did I seem to enjoy the prospect of being tied to a chair and receiving a working over by several brutal German policemen? I definitely have to stop spending so much time around Michael.

I entered the room and was escorted to a sofa and asked to sit down. In front of the sofa was a television. One of the policemen closed the door behind him and locked it. I was prepared for the worst. The other one came over and unlocked my handcuffs, turned the television on, and I was instantly presented with a bird's-eye view of the room I was just in, complete with sound of all the occupants.

I didn't get it and shrugged my shoulders at the policeman nearest me. The man didn't speak English, but reached into is pocket and handed me a note—which I read.

> *Dearest Robert,*
>
> *GOTCHA! I warned you not to think you could top me when it comes to practical jokes. But what I've done to you has a very serious side. I wanted you out of the room in case there's trouble, plus I was afraid you would guess the identity of the murderer before it was the proper time to do so and blurt it out. Another reason is that I'm planning a little revenge on your part. And finally, I know how you handle crises. So just sit back and enjoy the festivities for the next few minutes, all with the compliments of the surveillance system I finally found in a basement storage room.*
>
> *Monette*

Not since Ellen DeGeneres came out of the closet on prime-time television was I more glued to a set.

At first, no one said much of anything. I assumed they were too stunned. Julia, however, broke the silence.

"I thought he was the type to do it. He's got those shifty eyes, and he always has a look on his face like he hates you."

"Mother, I think he only does that with you," Michael reported. It was the most brilliant insight he'd had in his life.

"Well, when he came to stay at our house one night, I

felt he was going to steal some of the family silver, so I had all the good stuff locked up. But despite all my precautions, there still were a few pieces missing."

"*All* your precautions, Mrs. Stark?" Monette asked. "You just said you locked the silver up."

"I also had his baggage searched, just to make sure. After all, besides being a murderer, he's a thief also."

"And did you find anything, Julia?" Monette asked for clarification—and to allow Julia to hang herself some more.

"No, we couldn't find anything. But I swear, there are things missing," Mrs. Stark insisted.

"Could we continue?" Monette asked the crowd.

"Continue? I thought we were done!" Julia, Michael, and Ludwig said, almost in unison.

"No, no, we are not done. Actually, I think I have made a mistake. It was not Robert who killed the count. I think our answer lies in what happened at the party. Ludwig?" she asked, turning to our caftanned queen.

"Yes?" Ludwig responded, not without a little guilt showing on his red face.

"Your little party cost you a lot of money, yes?"

"All my parties take the money! I do not throw inexpensive parties!" Ludwig responded with a haughty air to set matters straight.

"That is exactly my point, Ludwig. The way you live costs a lot of money. Money which, I'm afraid, is almost gone."

All eyes shifted and became riveted on Ludwig.

"My money is not almost gone!" he said in defense.

"Well, if you have plenty of money, why were you borrowing from the count?"

"Me? Borrow money from Siegfreid? No! I said I have much money of my own! Why would you think I borrow the money from Siegfreid?"

"Because Robert overheard the count talking to you on the phone, saying you'd spent enough already. He also said he wouldn't give you any more money because you've made some bad mistakes and would have to live with them. Would you care to tell us what that was all about?"

Ludwig looked down at his lap as the table fell completely silent. Ludwig a murderer? I'd never expect a raving queen to be a *murderer*. I expect them to be *murdered*, yes. I can understand that. It seemed like an eternity before Ludwig began to confess.

"The other day, when you ask me to tell truth, I almost tell truth. Siegfreid and I do have a money arrangement. I . . . I . . ."—he spat out the words—"I . . . own part of a sex club in Bessenich, near Cologne. Siegfreid owned other half. We both put money to start this club, but it cost so much. We have to pay local government to open, to keep neighbors quiet, so many people to pay! It is a small town, very quiet, but a town with big costs. Another company own the club and Siegfreid and I own this company. No one can find out this way."

"A sex club? First, why? And second, why not open one in Berlin, much closer to where you and Siegfreid live?" Monette asked.

"The count and I want the club to give us the men and the sex. If we own club, the men who come are very nice to us. Why not Berlin? It is closer to Amsterdam, Paris, and London, and the people who come like to be quiet about them coming to this club, so small town is good. It is a secret—a secret that costs much money. This is what you hear when Siegfreid call to me on phone. I need the count to put more money to run club. I put up much. Now it is his turn to give more."

From the looks on Monette and Inspector Taucher's face, they didn't totally believe Ludwig's confession. Michael was more accepting.

"Where is this club located again?" he asked with a look on his face that said *I wish I had a pen just now.*

Julia, feeling her son had more than just a passing interest in Ludwig's sex club, shot daggers at Michael with her eyes.

Michael backtracked faster than a Texas savings and loan president. "Well, that sex club sounds disgusting! I'll just make a note never to go to a town like . . ."

"Bessenich," Monette said, giving Michael the information he was clearly seeking.

"Yes, Bessenich. Ugh!" Michael added, fooling absolutely no one.

Even from where I sat, I could see Monette was losing control of the audience, so she grabbed the reins and zeroed in on Ludwig once again. The bloodhound was on the trail.

"I guess for now, Ludwig, we will have to accept the story of your sex club. This is something we will look into. But there is something far more troubling about your connection to the count's death."

"Yes, ask me," Ludwig said, bracing himself.

"When I thought who could have murdered the count," Monette started, "I thought to myself, who was the last person to see the count alive? Was it Robert, who just left us abruptly? No, I said to myself. The first person to spot the body of the count was you, Ludwig!"

"But that does not make me murderer!" Ludwig replied.

"Ludwig, you told me when you saw the count's body stabbed and lying with his face in the toilet, you came out of the bathroom and screamed. Is that correct?"

"Yes, I see him and I scream."

"Apparently you scream a great deal, but let's not get into that," Monette stated, making fun of Ludwig without his even knowing it. "Anyway, Ludwig, how did you know it was Siegfreid in the bathroom stall if his head was in the toilet where you couldn't see his face?"

"I . . . I . . . know . . . his costume."

"But how did you know his costume? Everyone had a mask on, so how could you tell it was the count?"

"Well, the count . . . call me . . . he tell me what he was

wearing. This is how I know!" Ludwig answered with all the conviction of Rosemary Woods explaining how she had accidentally erased the Nixon White House tapes.

As all eyes fell on Ludwig, there was a tremendous clap of thunder outside, as if God himself was pointing the finger of accusation at Ludwig.

"Well," Michael commented, "I think we have our confirmation!"

There was dead silence. The two people on either side of Ludwig, Mrs. Stark and Uli Steben, the count's art dealer, slowly moved away from Ludwig.

"This cannot be!" exclaimed Ludwig. "I have no reason to kill Siegfreid. Why?"

"I don't know. But thank you for *finally* being honest about the sex club, Ludwig. That helps me make up my mind here about one little thing that has been bothering me. But there are other things that bother me far more, and I will now tell you about them.

"After the count was murdered, Robert and I discovered surveillance videotapes in a servant's room in the basement of this house—thanks to Michael Stark here."

Michael looked like lightning was about to strike him. And it could have if Monette cared to elucidate on exactly how we found those tapes. But she was a lesbian on a mission, so she continued.

"On those tapes were hours and hours of Siegfreid sitting, eating, entertaining guests, going about his daily life here in the house. My question was why? Second question. Over and over again, people said Siegfreid was, and I quote, a prick—*der penis*—when he was was absolutely charming to Robert and me. Why the difference? Third question. In this folder is the coroner's report on Count Siegfreid von Schmidt. In it, it states that Siegfreid's eye color is blue—when his eyes were green."

Everyone sitting around the table was silent, presumably

lost in thought trying to answer the three questions. Monette, however, didn't give them enough time.

"The answer, gentlemen, is that the count killed the count!" she said with dramatic heaviness.

The whole table looked completely puzzled. The guests looked back and forth amongst themselves, seeking some kind of answer. Then all eyes turned in Monette's direction, pleading for her to make some kind of sense.

"I don't get it," Michael said—of all people. "How could the count kill himself? You mean it was a suicide?"

Everyone turned from Michael to Monette. It was like watching a verbal tennis game, with all heads turning toward whomever was doing the talking.

"There were two counts all the time. The real one, and an impostor. But let me digress for a moment. Like I said before, the beginnings of this murder started over a year ago. The count had a lover by the name of Hans Sattler. The count was so in love with Hans that he made out a will that gave half of his entire fortune to Hans and the other half to Heino, his business partner.

"Eventually, the two lovers parted, but Siegfreid failed to change his will. After all, why bother? The count was young and healthy. But his lover rightly feared that someday the count would change his will. So Hans began to plan.

"Hans thought if Siegfreid died before the will was changed, he would inherit half of everything. And that was true. But he probably reasoned any premature death would be suspicious and he would look like the guilty party. So he came up with an idea that would throw suspicion on another person, yet lead to Siegfreid's death, thus killing two birds with one stone. Hans found a man who needed money desperately and who bore a close resemblance to Siegfreid von Schmidt. This man's name was Manfred.

"Manfred, you see, didn't have to be a dead ringer, since the count always wore sunglasses and frequently changed his appearance, so an exact impostor wasn't necessary. The key was to get the impostor seen out and about as much as was possible without exposing him—all to make him seem legitimate to Robert and everyone else. Hans then used his friendship to gain entrance to the count's palace, where he placed remote surveillance cameras to capture the count on videotape. What Herr Sattler wanted were tapes of Siegfreid eating, gesturing, entertaining, talking on the phone so that Manfred could learn the mannerisms that would make people believe he was the real count. When Manfred was ready to imitate Siegfreid, the two overpowered the count and imprisoned him in Hans's apartment and Manfred, the impostor, went about firing the palace staff and hiring completely new servants to eliminate the possibility of anyone recognizing that the count wasn't the real count."

There was a knock on the door to the dining room, and in stepped two policemen with a third man in handcuffs.

"Ah, what good timing," Monette commented. "This is Manfred, everyone. He not only lived in this house in the room where we found the videotapes, but if you look beyond his freshly shaved head, you will notice his resemblance to the late Siegfreid von Schmidt. Manfred, would you please sit down and join us? Not that you have much choice."

Monette waited until Manfred was helped into a chair by his two guards before she plowed on.

"What happened next is pure conjecture on my part, but here goes. Hans needed someone to frame with a phony will scheme and it needed to be someone in another country who would know little about Siegfreid. I suppose you saw the article in *Vanity Fair* magazine last year," she said, turning to Manfred, "the one about how Michael Stark was implicated in the murder of a boyfriend and how he and Robert *and* I solved the case?"

"Yes," Manfred admitted. "As I read the article, Robert's

comments proved I couldn't find a more gullible person if I tried, and none more desperate for love than Mr. Willsop. He was perfect."

I couldn't believe Manfred admitted his plot so readily, but when the jig is up, the jig is up.

"Now, Manfred flies to New York, arranges to be in the same restaurant as the desperate-for-love Robert, and woos him silly. They make love several times every day," Monette said, smiling.

She continued. "He takes Robert everywhere, but still follows his cardinal rule: avoid close contact with anyone who knows the real count. In New York, this is not as much of a problem as it is in Germany. There's even a bon voyage party for Robert, thrown by the count and attended by many of the count's friends. Or are they? I was lucky to be given a business card from one of the women at the party and found out she was hired to act like she was a friend of the count. The woman—and everyone else at the party— never laid eyes on the count before that night. You see, she and a lot of others were told the count wanted to assure his new boyfriend he had many friends in America and if they played the part at the party, Robert would feel better about moving to Germany. The thing that tipped me off was that several people at the party kept asking who the count was— as if they had no idea.

"Are you still with me?" Monette asked and got a round of heads nodding in agreement. "Just stay seated, because this story *does* have an ending. Robert agrees to move to Germany, and as they are going through customs, agent Ralf Reimann sees Siegfried's passport and asks the count to remove his ever present sunglasses. What does he find? He finds that the count's eye color is green, not blue as it shows on Siegfried's passport. Even Robert mentioned the count's eyes were green, but didn't know what color the real count's eyes were, since he always wore sunglasses. I only discovered they were green myself when someone at Ludwig's party bumped into the count and knocked off his mask. Plus, Robert had the sheer luck to have visited an optometrist in New York that just hours before Manfred, posing as the count, visited to get a prescription for contact lenses filled."

Julia, who was probably thinking how much I could sue her for libel, spoke up. "So?"

"It was a fact that few people would have known, but the real Siegfreid von Schmidt had 20/20 vision. He didn't need contacts. Right, Manfred?" Monette asked. "But you did buy some contacts in New York. Tinted blue I suspect?"

"Yes, but I couldn't wear them . . . they hurt my eyes," Manfred answered. "I don't wear them either, but we needed my eyes to look blue. I eventually stopped wearing the contacts, figuring that no one would notice my green eyes behind my sunglasses."

"Ah," Monette added in triumph, "but people did . . . including R. Reimann. Anyway, it was incredibly bad luck for the count to run into Herr Reimann, because this particular customs agent had another part-time job. He would blackmail people coming through customs by either planting contraband in their luggage, or he would find something that could get the traveler in trouble with the law.

"The impostor count—I'm sorry, Manfred—thinks he has fooled the customs man until Ralf shows up at Siegfreid's house a day or two later to demand money, which threatens the entire plan that Manfred and Hans have worked so hard to carry off. Manfred arranges to go to Monaco with Robert while Hans stays behind at the palace to receive Herr Reimann, who is murdered and put into a freezer in the second basement in this house. And this is the part where Karl could help us shed a little light on why he was here in the house the same time Ralf was killed—a time when he should have been on vacation."

Karl looked up in surprise and protested loudly, "I do not

come back to house until da count, he return from Monte Carlo!"

"Karl," Monette explained, "Inspector Taucher has found out you bought a train ticket to return you to Berlin on the day we believe Ralf Reimann was killed. I think you'd better be honest, because you are in hot *wasser* right now."

"OK, OK, I come here mit boyfreund! We use da house to haf zex in, if you must know!"

"Karl, I need a truthful response to this question. As you and your boyfriend were having sex in this house, did you notice anyone else here?"

"We do not zee anyvun here, but ven ve come to house, there vas two car outside. Later, vee taut ve hear somevun in house, but then we listen and nutting!"

"Did you look outside into the courtyard later to see if the two cars were there?"

"Yah."

"And?" Monette requested.

"Dere vas no cars there."

"Thank you, Karl. You have answered another question that mystified me. Why would Hans keep the body of Ralf in this house? Why not get rid of both him and his car at the same time? The answer is, Hans was planning to, but Karl's unexpected appearance at the house forced Hans to change his plans. He put the body in the basement freezer and, I expect, drove Ralf's car away and abandoned it on the streets of Berlin. But let us get back to the story.

"During Robert's entire time in Europe, Manfred keeps Robert away from other people by having nonstop sex, which the pathetic Robert is all too eager to oblige," Monette said, looking up into the camera and smiling to me. Another gotcha. "Manfred and Robert return from Monaco and attend Ludwig's masquerade ball—the perfect place for the impostor to gain more credibility of being the real count, yet not be exposed. It's also the perfect place to make the switch back to the real count in order to finally kill him. The impostor is seen getting progressively drunker, when in reality he is not drunk at all. The point being when the real count—who has been forced to get drunk—is brought from Hans's apartment and into the ball by Hans, he will be cooperative and not believed should he ask for help. Manfred has sex in a linen closet with Robert, then excuses himself on the pretext that he is going to vomit . . ."

"Not that this would be an unusual reaction to seeing Robert naked," Michael said.

I made another in a long series of mental notes to get back at Michael in the worst way possible.

Monette snorted a small laugh and continued, " . . . as I said, excuses himself at a prearranged time and disappears out the door, ditching the persona of the count forever. The real Siegfreid is led into the ball by Hans, who has secured an invitation for himself and a guest somehow. Hans leads the count to the bathroom, puts his head in the toilet, stabs him in the back, and leaves. Robert comes down to the bathroom and has the sheer bad luck to enter just moments after the count was killed. When Michael reveals he was made the main beneficiary in the count's will, the finger of blame is pointed right at Robert."

Ludwig asked the question that was on even my mind, but not quite in my words. "So if Hans Sattler is man who murdered Siegfreid, why are you here? Should you not go find him?"

"We don't have to," Monette replied. "He's sitting right here," she said, motioning to Uli Steben with a Carol-Merrill wave of her hand. Uli—I mean Hans—flashed a *who, me?* look at Monette and burst from his chair as if he were spring-loaded. His explosive attempt at escape surprised even Herr Taucher, who was knocked backward as Hans made for one of the windows. It looked like he might have made his escape if it weren't for the most unlikely hero in the world: Ludwig. To be honest, it wasn't Ludwig per se who stopped Siegfried's murderer from perhaps making an escape. It was the voluminous caftan Ludwig was wearing. As Hans ran, he tripped on the caftan and went down faster than a round of German beer at Octoberfest. Several policemen heard the scuffle from down the hall and entered the room, subduing Hans with handcuffs and lifting him into a sitting position in one of the chairs so Monette could finish her story.

Monette then looked directly into the camera and told me it was OK for me to come back to the dining room. When I returned, Michael exclaimed he was so happy I didn't murder the count. Julia was pretty much silent—not even an apology for her earlier assassination of my character. I sat down at the table and asked a question that was on my mind for some time.

"Monette, how did you know that Uli and Hans were the same person?"

"Process of elimination really. That, plus a little deductive reasoning. Remember when you and I went to spy on Uli in New York and found out no one in the art world had heard of him? Then Inspector Taucher can't turn up anything on him either. So it stands to reason that Uli is a fictional character made up by someone with a big stake in this whole affair. So I think to myself, this murder isn't about revenge—there's too much money at stake. Who stands to gain the most from Siegfried's death? Two people! Heio and Hans. So Taucher checks the movements of both and what do you know? Only Hans was in New York at the same time the count was—on business, supposedly. Plus, there's another clue that tipped me off that Uli and Hans were the same person. Actually you noticed it."

I was baffled. "I don't understand what it is I saw."

"You noticed how well-dressed Uli was—almost too well dressed. Me too. Impeccable was the word you used. Well, guess what Hans does for a living?"

"He works for a fashion house in Düsseldorf!" I answered, now understanding all. "Now I have another question. When the police went to Hans's apartment today to bring him here to the inquiry, how did you get Hans to masquerade as Uli? He hasn't played that part for some time now."

"Easy. I knew that Manfred would be there, so I instructed the police to knock on Hans's door and to ask for Uli Steben. Thankfully, Hans answered the door and was so thrown for a loop that the police had made some connection between him and the character of Uli, he slipped into the role of Herr Steben. He would just have to figure some way out of the part of Uli later. Manfred, seeing what was going on, pretend he was Hans Sattler for the moment. The police then came to the count's house with Uli. Both knew something was up, so as soon as the police left with Uli (or Hans), Manfred bolted the apartment and headed for the airport—with the police following him the whole way and stopping him before he could get on a plane.

"I guess there's little more to add. I just want to thank you all for coming and helping us catch these two murderers. Inspector, I think you can take Hans and Manfred away."

"No, wait," I shouted as I jumped up from my chair and ran around to confront the man who had deceived me and set me up for the crime of murder.

"Robert, remember that kicking a suspect in the balls is not a good idea," Monette warned me.

"No worry," I said to Monette, determined to keep my head held up high. I turned back to Manfred. "Just one question. Did you ever love me?"

Manfred raised his humbled head and looked me straight in the eye. "In the beginning, Robert, you were just part of our plan. But the more time I spent with you, the more I really liked you. I even began to love you."

The police grabbed Manfred by the arm to escort him away, but I stopped them one more time.

"And what about the sex?" I asked, fully prepared for the answer.

Manfred looked at me one last time. "There was no faking there. It was the most enjoyable of my life."

I had my answer. I had my confirmation. A smile welled up inside me and overtook my face. I looked at Michael to make sure he'd heard what Manfred said. The look—and the smile—on his face said he did.

The spell seemed to linger in the air as Hans and Manfred were led away.

I shook my head to bring me out of my state. "Monette, I still think I could have handled the situation, but I'm grateful for my bird's-eye view."

"We've been over that, Robert. You're about as useful in a stressful situation as Joan Rivers is on a camping trip. I didn't know what Hans was going to do. Well, I guess it's back to the perfume counter at Black's for you," she said, quoting a line from my favorite movie of all time, *The Women*.

"I guess you're right, Monette," I said, trying to salvage one of the most fucked-up adventures I have ever had in my life. "Well, at least I still have my crummy apartment to come home to—and this beautiful Rolex watch and a gorgeous car. It wasn't a complete loss!"

I started to leave the room, but Monette grabbed me by the arm and pulled me back. "Uh, Robert, I hate to tell you this, but Herr Taucher wants you to return anything Manfred bought you with the count's money. They can't expect you to make amends for everything spent, but you're going to have to hand over the watch and the car as evidence."

"Can't anything good ever happen to me?" I cried, realizing that, once again, life had dealt me an entire hand of jokers. "You know, I try to do unto others as I'd have them do unto me, I'm kind and respectful—and this is the thanks

I get! Shit!" I said, begrudgingly peeling the watch from my resistant arm and handing it to Herr Taucher.

I don't know whether I was in shock or lost in thought, but Monette turned to me and asked me what was wrong.

"Oh, nothing—if you don't count the fact that for months, I was sleeping with not only a murderer, but a complete stranger!"

Michael who was silent until now, looked at me and said, "I know it feels weird, Robert, but in time you'll get used to it. I ought to know!"

17

Click Your Heels Together Three Times and Those Big Shiny Boots Will Take You Home

The next day, we found ourselves packing to take a noon flight back to New York. Julia, the woman who had falsely accused me in front of a dozen people, was leaving two hours earlier to take a flight into Boston.

"I can't believe that fucking Julia," I complained to Monette. "She never apologized to me for accusing me of murder. I wonder if I can sue her for libel? I could use a few hundred thousand dollars," I said, slipping a few towels into my suitcase, compliments of the count. If I couldn't have my Rolex or my car, at least I'd have something that would fit in my tiny apartment.

"Forget it, Robert. You'd never win because she'd have better lawyers."

"I guess you're right. I just wish there was some way to get back at her."

"I can't believe you're admitting defeat. You've played some of the most devious pranks on me, Monette Mastermind, and you're letting that self-centered Marie Antoinette get the best of you? For shame, Robert, for shame!"

I was stuffing more towels into my suitcase when Michael passed by the door, bearing two suitcases.

"Michael, where were you last night? I saw you drag in at six A.M.," I reported.

"Oh, out . . . taking care of a few things," he answered evasively.

"What were their names?" Monette asked.

"I said I was just out taking care of some unfinished business," Michael explained.

"You didn't take Robert's Mercedes last night, did you?" Monette inquired of Michael. "Herr Taucher sent a tow truck over this morning to retrieve the car, and it's not in the front drive anymore. Plus someone left the gate in the front of the house open."

"Don't look at me, I haven't seen the car. I took a cab last night. Someone must have stolen it."

"Maybe it's better that someone probably took it. That way I don't have to sit and watch the Berlin police department tow away everything I ever got from the count." I tried to change gears. "So where are you going so soon?" I asked Michael. "The flight isn't until noon, so we've got plenty of time."

"Oh, these aren't my suitcases. These are my mother's. She asked me to put her coat from the front hall closet into her suitcase, lock it, and take it out front for the cab driver to load. Her cab's supposed to be here any minute."

Monette and I looked at each other, reading each other's twisted minds. It was at times like these that I realized how much Monette and I thought alike.

"Michael," Julia's voice called from the other end of the hall, "could you come here a minute? I need some help closing this carry-on bag."

"I'll be right back," Michael said and scurried off to the Evil Queen of Newport.

It only took a minute to accomplish our task, so when Michael returned and grabbed the suitcases, Monette and I were quite happy we had proved that while justice may be exceedingly blind and unbiased, it can also be vengeful.

Julia stopped by to bid a perfunctory farewell and told us it was a pleasure knowing us. I was about to shake the cadaverous hand she extended to me, but I doubled over with laughter and couldn't stop. I could see Monette was trying to keep herself from laughing also, her face turning red in the effort.

"Well, good-bye," Julia said and was gone.

Monette and I were still laughing when the limousine came to fetch us and take us to the airport.

We continued to laugh for at least the first hour of the flight back to New York.

"I wish I was there when Julia opened her suitcase at the Berlin airport and found that three-foot dildo!" I said, gasping for breath. "Oh God, I bet she was surprised!"

"Your idea was brilliant, Robert!" she said, the laughter finally ebbing to a chuckle. "I couldn't have done it better myself. Plus, there's a certain elegance in the way the dildo has traveled full circle."

"Monette, you deserve some of the credit. Putting all that metal in her suitcase meant she would have to open it at check in!"

While the laughing calmed considerably as the in-flight movie began, every once in a while we would look at each other and burst into laughter all over again. Michael, who was sitting across the aisle from us in first class (which, incidentally, he paid for), couldn't figure out what we were laughing about and decided to tune us out with his movie headphones.

As the plane crossed over England and headed out over the Atlantic, the only thought I had was that I hoped Mrs. Stark would make good use of her souvenir from Germany.

*   *   *

Once I was ensconced back in my roach-infested apartment and had secured my old job again (no one wanted it), I thought about going back to Germany and actually seeing the country. But not right away. Things had to cool down a bit.

It's not that I was afraid of being implicated in the count's murder. Herr Taucher said I could completely forget about it—which I tried, but I had to admit I felt a certain amount of guilt. This guilt rose up in me every time I drove the Mercedes Michael had spirited out of Germany and shipped to the U.S. for me, using his endless sexual and financial connections.

Michael got an even bigger kick that he had shipped the contraband car on one of Siegfreid's boats. But even a do-gooder like Monette told me that in time I would feel better. But in the meantime, she wisely counseled me to keep the car in a garage far out in the rolling hills of Bucks County, Pennsylvania, where I would drive it on weekends.

As I roared down the winding country roads, I had to admit that despite the fact my situation in Germany looked a little bleak at one point, there was a lot of good that came out of the entire affair. Ludwig personally invited me to his party next year, and I had to admit the sex I had with Manfred was pretty great. But besides the car, I did manage to hold on to one other memento from my adventure in Germany: the ring Manfred gave me. I held on to that—just because.